CW00854100

Incantations and Iced Coffee - A Coffee Witch Cozy Mystery – Maddie Goodwell 6

by

Jinty James

Incantations and Iced Coffee – A
Coffee Witch Cozy Mystery – Maddie
Goodwell 6

by

Jinty James

This is a work of fiction. All
characters, names, places and events are
the product of the author's imagination or
used fictitiously.

CHAPTER 1

"Phew!" Suzanne Taylor wiped her brow, her strawberry-blonde ponytail looking limp. "It's hot!" Her white t-shirt and denim shorts looked rumpled and wilted already.

"I know." Maddie Goodwell sighed as she slid an iced coffee over to her friend to decorate with whipped cream. She didn't think her t-shirt and shorts looked any better. And her brown shoulder-length hair felt just the tiniest bit damp.

"Broomf!" Trixie, Maddie's familiar, scrunched up her furry white face in agreement. With her turquoise eyes, white coat, and silver spine and tail, the Persian did not look her usual contented self.

Suzanne took the cup from Maddie, icy droplets of condensation forming on the plastic sides, squirted a large amount of cream on it, and handed it to their customer, a teenage girl whose eyes lit up as she took her first sip.

"Thanks guys!" she waved as she headed across the town square.

"Maybe you should have stayed home, Trixie." Maddie turned around as she spoke to the cat. "It might be cooler there." Trixie sat on her usual stool in their coffee truck, Brewed from the Bean.

"Broomf," Trixie grumbled, settling down on the stool.

"Maybe she doesn't want to miss out on seeing her favorite customers," Suzanne suggested.

"Mrrow." Trixie seemed to nod her head in agreement.

"Make sure you tell me if you do want to go home," Maddie told her familiar.

"Mrrow," the feline replied softly, her eyes closing in what appeared to be a snooze.

Maddie hoped Trixie's fluffy white fur wouldn't make her too hot. Although they had a fan going on in the rear of the truck and the windows and back door were open, it was still a little warm inside.

Maddie couldn't remember such hot weather in July before in Estherville, a small town one hundred miles from Seattle.

"Maybe Trixie's thinking of a cooling spell." Suzanne gazed hopefully at the cat.

Maddie frowned. Although Trixie had helped her out of some tight spots, *such as being face to face with a killer,* she didn't think Trixie had done any spells when it *wasn't* a dangerous situation.

"Do you really think …" Maddie's voice trailed off as the temperature in the truck lowered by a couple of degrees.

"She is!" Suzanne stared at the Persian in delight.

"Shh." Maddie looked out through the serving hatch, but for the moment they didn't have any customers, which was just as well. Nobody knew about Trixie's – or Maddie's – talents.

Ever since she was seven years old, when she bought a crumbling book from the local secondhand bookstore called *Wytchcraft for the Chosen*, Maddie had been able to see the future – or the possible future – in the next twenty-four hours, on the surface of a freshly made coffee. It didn't matter if it was instant, drip, latte, or iced coffee she now made in their coffee truck.

About eighteen months ago, Trixie had come into her life, and they'd been inseparable ever since. There was something magical about Trixie. Maddie couldn't define it, but she had no doubts. Trixie was *special*.

When Maddie turned twenty-seven – or seven-and-twenty as the ancient tome had stated, her world began to change. With Trixie's help, Maddie had been able to execute *new* spells – so far at the rate of one per month, after each full moon. The spells had helped Maddie, Trixie, and Suzanne solve their first murder. Maddie's personal life had changed, too. She was now dating Luke, Suzanne's brother, whom she'd been crushing on for years.

The temperature fell another notch and Maddie drew in a big breath.

"That feels wonderful, Trix." She studied the cat. "Are you doing that?"

"Mrrow!" Trixie opened her eyes, looking pleased. She also looked a lot cooler.

"Keep doing it, Trix," Suzanne urged, smiling at the Persian.

"Mrrow," Trixie answered, closing her eyes again.

"Putting iced coffee on the menu was a great idea," Maddie said to Suzanne, her best friend since middle school, and the only person who knew about her and Trixie.

"Thanks!" Suzanne's ponytail bounced slightly. "I don't blame people for not wanting to drink something hot in this weather – or even buy one of my health balls – but we need to make sure our sales don't decline."

"Our customers seem to like the lemon water as well," Maddie said, gesturing to the refrigerator. Their new line was almost sold out already, and it was nearly noon.

"Since there aren't any customers at the moment—" Suzanne peered through the serving hatch "—why don't we make ourselves an iced coffee? I didn't have time for one this morning."

"Good idea." Maddie set to work, the machine grinding and hissing. A couple of minutes later, she set down Suzanne's coffee in front of her. "Maybe you should put your cream on yourself – I know you like a lot."

"You bet I do." Suzanne giggled, her mood more upbeat since Trixie had cooled down the truck. A *shhhhh* noise ensued as she squirted a mound of cream on top of her icy drink.

"Wow." Maddie's eyes widened. She'd allowed herself a modest amount of cream on top of her beverage, but it was nothing compared to Suzanne's.

Just as they sat down to enjoy their iced concoctions, the sound of clanging caught their attention. Maddie had just taken a sip, the frosty caffeine giving her a welcome energy boost, but she put down her drink as her curiosity impelled her to look out of the serving hatch.

"No way!" She beckoned to Suzanne. "Look!"

"What the?!" It wasn't like Suzanne to be lost for words.

"Mrrow??" Trixie enquired.

"It's Claudine," Maddie said grimly.

"And she better not be doing what it looks like she's doing." Suzanne glowered at the previously empty space next to their truck in the town square. A space that now hosted Claudine Claxton, a large table, and a sign.

Claudine was their nemesis who ran the café on the other side of the square and who was Maddie's former boss. Until Maddie, Suzanne, and Trixie started up their own business – Brewed from the Bean.

"Brrrr," Trixie grumbled, her ears flattening at the sound of the clanging. The temperature in the van warmed slightly.

"Oh no." Suzanne's mouth turned down. "It's getting warmer in here!"

"It's okay, Trix." Maddie spoke gently. "Don't worry about Claudine." She knew the feline didn't like the other woman either – Trixie's first run in with Maddie's former boss was when Trixie had come into the coffee shop, looking lost. Claudine had threatened the cat before Maddie had taken Trixie home with her – and they'd been inseparable ever since.

"Broomf," Trixie muttered, before settling down on the stool and closing her eyes. The temperature slowly dropped again.

"I'm going to see what that sign says." Suzanne marched out of the truck.

Maddie put down her iced coffee and joined her friend, her stomach sinking when she was close enough to read the homemade sign.

Iced Coffee.

A large pitcher of a black liquid, which Maddie assumed to be the coffee, was on one side of the table, while a pile of plastic cups was on the other.

The one good thing was that there weren't any customers – yet.

"Oh no, you don't." Suzanne fisted her hands on her hips as she stared at Claudine. "You are *not* setting up next to us."

"It's a free country." Claudine's whining nasal voice assaulted Maddie's eardrums. "I can do what I like."

"I don't think you can," Maddie said politely, although she seethed inside. "We have permission from the town for our truck. Do you?"

The stout forty-something woman dressed in a black shirt and culottes shrugged as if she couldn't care less.

"One taste of my coffee and they'll be hooked."

"I doubt it," Suzanne said, looking at the pitcher of inky black liquid. "If that's what you'll be serving."

"What's wrong with it?" Claudine glared at her. "It's got ice and coffee in it. Iced coffee. Anyway—" she tossed her head, her black bob not moving by a strand, "—I can sell iced coffee if you can."

"Who's managing the café?" Maddie asked. Somehow, despite Claudine's unsunny nature, bad coffee, and stale pastries, she still had a trickle of customers.

"My cousin Veronica." Claudine smiled genuinely for a second. It was an unfamiliar sight. "She arrived last night and is visiting for a while. She grew up here, you know."

"No, we didn't know," Suzanne said, exchanging a surprised glance with Maddie.

"Of course, she's older than me," Claudine continued, setting out some plastic cups. "But while she's here she's going to help me out."

"That's nice," Maddie said faintly, wondering what Veronica was like. An older version of Claudine? Or someone completely different?"

"Get your iced coffee here!" Claudine suddenly hollered, causing Maddie and Suzanne to flinch and step backward. *"Iced coffee right here!"*

A couple of passersby stopped and looked at Claudine's table, then shook their heads and hurried past.

"I hope you're not going to be shouting all afternoon," Suzanne told the older woman. "Otherwise, you're going to scare away our customers."

"Your customers will be *my* customers," Claudine informed her, a smirk on her face. "One sip is all they'll need – and they'll come to my café from now on."

"In your dreams." Suzanne sniffed, swiveled, and stalked back to the truck, the familiar graphic of brown coffee beans dancing on the outside of the truck not seeming to cheer her up.

Maddie followed, casting a worried glance over her shoulder at Claudine. She didn't have any customers – yet.

"What are we going to do?" Maddie asked once they returned to the truck. She kept her voice down. There was no way she wanted her nemesis to hear her concern.

"I don't know what we *can* do," Suzanne said slowly, furrowing her brow.

The temperature in the truck was just as cool as when they'd left, which was the only good thing at the moment.

"Mrrow?" Trixie opened her eyes, blinking at them.

"Iced coffee!" Maddie heard Claudine's loud nasal voice and winced.

"I'm not going to listen to *that* for the rest of the day." Suzanne shook her head in disgust and stomped out of the truck. "Shoo!" she waved her hands at Claudine, as if the older woman were a stray animal. "Go away!"

"Make me." Claudine smirked. She didn't appear to have any customers, though.

"Suzanne." Maddie tugged her friend's arm. "Let's get back in the truck."

"Better listen to her," Claudine called. "Because I'm not budging."

Suzanne stalked back to the truck and plopped down on a stool.

"Iced Coffee!"

"Gahhh!" Suzanne clutched her head.

"Mrrow?" Trixie looked at the girl with widened eyes.

"I think you're worrying Trixie." Maddie glanced at her friend in concern.

Suzanne smiled weakly at the cat. "I'm okay, Trix. But that woman just *affects* me! I don't know how you can stay so calm, Mads."

"I'm not calm on the inside," Maddie said wryly. "But I had to learn not to let her get to me when I worked for her, or my work day would have been even worse."

"I know," Suzanne said sympathetically.

"Maybe she'll give up if she doesn't have many customers." Maddie tried to look on the bright side. "In the meantime, since it's quiet, I think we should eat our lunch."

"Good idea." Suzanne cheered up slightly.

They grabbed their lunch from the fridge. Maddie shook some dry food into one of Trixie's special bowls, but the Persian didn't seem interested.

After they ate their sandwiches, business picked up a little. Maddie was relieved to see that their customers didn't seem tempted to investigate Claudine's icy offering.

"How can that woman even think that she's selling acceptable iced coffee?" Suzanne grumbled when the last of their lunchtime customers had departed.

Claudine's constant cries of, *"Iced Coffee!"* had lessened somewhat. Maddie wondered if the other woman was becoming hoarse.

"I know," Maddie agreed. "We give people the option of milk and whipped cream as well as just coffee and ice."

"And her coffee is *terrible*." Suzanne shuddered. "I can't imagine her using different beans to the ones she uses in her café."

"Let's hope she gets bored and packs up her table," Maddie said, hoping her wish would come true.

***

It didn't.

The next day, after the early morning rush, Claudine arrived and set up her table next to their truck.

"Oh no." Suzanne's mouth tightened. "Not again!"

"Broomf!" Trixie hopped on the counter and peered out of the serving hatch, something she usually didn't do. "Broomf!"

The day was a little cooler than the day before – thank goodness. But Trixie did *not* look happy. The Persian shook herself, her fluffy white fur settling back into place immediately. She turned and hopped over to her stool, hunching down on the wooden seat.

Nobody had batted an eye at Trixie appearing in the coffee truck from time to time. Not even the health inspector, after Maddie had first opened for business, but Trixie seemed to know without being told not to go near the counter or the coffee machines. She must really be annoyed at Claudine's presence.

"Hello, Maddie and Suzanne." The mayor, Larry Clawdell, appeared at the counter. "And Trixie." He smiled at the feline.

"Mrrow," Trixie sat up straight as she greeted the middle-aged man. She seemed to like the mayor, who had given them permission to operate Brewed from the Bean in the town square.

"Hi, Larry." Suzanne greeted him.

"Iced coffee!" Claudine hollered.

"Hi." Maddie gave him a strained smile. "Would you like a coffee?"

"I'd love my usual, Maddie." He dug into his pocket for his wallet.

"One triple latte coming up." Maddie set to work, the machine grinding and hissing as it extracted the liquor from the beans. She was tempted to do a Coffee Vision spell with the mayor's coffee, but decided now wasn't the right time. Not with Claudine's constant yelling in the background.

"I've had a complaint," the mayor said as Suzanne handed him his coffee.

Maddie and Suzanne stared at each other.

"Oh?" Maddie found her voice.

"It's about Ms. Claxton." The mayor gestured to their nemesis, sitting behind her temporary table next to their truck. "Is she bothering you?"

"You bet she is!" Suzanne's ponytail bobbed in the affirmative.

"Broomf!" Trixie scrunched up her face, in agreeance with Suzanne.

"That's what I was afraid of." He grimaced. "She doesn't have permission to operate next to you – in fact, she shouldn't be conducting business outside her café. I'll have to tell her to shut it down."

"Thank goodness." Suzanne gave the mayor a relieved smile. "I ended up with a headache yesterday afternoon with her constant shouting of—" Suzanne's words were cut off.

"Iced coffee!"

"Broomf!" Trixie sounded cross.

"That settles it," the mayor said. "We can't have Trixie upset, can we?"

Maddie was sure she saw out of the corner of her eye Trixie shake her head no. Right now, nothing would surprise her about her familiar.

"No, we can't," Maddie jumped in. "Thank you, Larry."

"How's business otherwise?" he asked.

"Pretty good – or it was until *you know*," Suzanne jerked her head toward Claudine's stand. "Our iced coffees were selling well."

"And I'm sure they will again," the mayor said. "Don't worry, Trixie, Claudine will go back to her café now."

"Mrrow." Trixie sounded as if she were saying *"Thank you."*

Maddie and Suzanne leaned out of the serving hatch as the mayor walked over to Claudine's table. He said something to the woman which made her scowl and cast a fierce glare at their truck. After another minute of heated conversation, Claudine gathered up her plastic cups and pitcher of iced caffeine, looking like she wanted to pour it over the mayor's head.

"It's not fair!" they heard her tell the mayor. "They're here. Why can't I be here?"

"Because you can't," the mayor told her, looking uncomfortable at her display of temper. "If you want to apply for a permit, then fill in the paperwork and submit it. But you already have your café on the other side of the square."

"You won't hear the last of this!" Claudine shook her finger at him as she stomped toward her café, leaving her table behind.

"Phew!" Suzanne flopped on a stool. "I'm glad that's over."

"I hope it is," Maddie said, watching Claudine depart. The mayor also seemed to be watching the older woman head toward her café, before turning around and giving Maddie a wave as he left the square.

"She'll probably send one of her employees to pack up her table," Suzanne said, stroking Trixie.

"Probably," Maddie replied. To her knowledge, Claudine only employed one part-time barista.

"I wonder who made the complaint?" Suzanne furrowed her brow. "Whoever it is, we owe them a drink on the house!"

"We certainly do," Maddie agreed.

"Mrrow," Trixie purred.

"Aren't we lucky the mayor has a soft spot for you, Trix?" Suzanne continued stroking the feline. "Otherwise …"

"We might not have been so fortunate," Maddie said ruefully. She paused as a sudden thought struck her. "Trixie, you didn't use any magic on the mayor, did you?" She kept her voice down, even though there weren't any customers in sight.

"Mrrow!" Trixie sounded affronted at the idea.

"Well, I didn't *really* think so," Maddie replied to her familiar.

"But wouldn't it have been cool if she had?" Suzanne's eyes sparkled. "I wish I had magical powers like you two."

"I don't have that many," Maddie said ruefully. "Apart from the Coffee Vision spell."

"And the Tell the Truth spell, Escape Your Enemy, Move an Object—"

"Okay, okay," Maddie said hastily. She loved Suzanne, but her best friend could get a little carried away. Sometimes Maddie worried that one day someone would overhear them talking about magic and either tell the whole town or want to know more. Maddie didn't want to deal with either possibility.

Her parents didn't know she had magical abilities.

Neither did her boyfriend, Luke.

She knew she should tell him sometime, but they hadn't been dating that long. He was Suzanne's older brother, so she'd first met him when she'd been in middle school, but their relationship was new and something she didn't want to endanger by telling him the one thing about her – and Trixie – that he didn't know.

But she didn't want to have to hide it from him forever – did she?

An influx of customers kept her busy for the rest of the morning. Since Claudine's stand had been shut down, they had more orders for iced coffee than they'd had yesterday afternoon – something Maddie was grateful for.

By the end of the day, she was beat. Suzanne must have felt the same way because she flopped on a stool as soon as they closed the serving hatch in the late afternoon.

Trixie snoozed on her stool, seeming content now that nobody – such as Claudine – was shouting their wares.

Maddie just hoped that tomorrow everything would go back to normal – plenty of customers and no Claudine.

CHAPTER 2

Maddie's hope turned out to be wishful thinking.

The next day started out like any normal weekday. Trixie had decided to stay at home. The Persian came to work with her most days, but sometimes she seemed to need a day to herself.

Maddie knew the feeling.

Maddie – and Suzanne – kept an eye on Trixie when she was home alone by checking the live camera feed on Maddie's phone. Mostly, Trixie sat on the sofa and guarded *Wytchcraft for the Chosen*, Maddie's ancient spell book.

The morning rush went smoothly, although some of their customers remarked on Trixie's absence, and asked Maddie to say hello to her for them.

Maddie and Suzanne had decided to buy their lunch for a change, from the salad shop across the square. Maddie felt guilty for closing the truck for ten minutes, but they'd agreed that they deserved a short break, especially after the events of the past two days.

"Maybe we should cross to the other side of the street," Maddie said as they neared Claudine's café, a cool breeze ruffling her hair.

"Nonsense," Suzanne replied briskly. "She didn't have a problem setting up right next to us yesterday or the day before, so why should we be afraid of walking past her coffee shop? We have a perfect right to use this bit of sidewalk, just like everyone else in town." Suzanne straightened her spine and marched ahead, as if daring anyone to stop her.

"It's just a feeling," Maddie murmured. Sometimes she received whispers of intuition – another aspect of her modest witchy abilities.

They reached Claudine's café without incident. Just as they were about to walk past the entrance, the door opened with a rush.

"Stop right there!" Claudine emerged from the shop with a glower on her face. "I want a word with you two!"

"Me too!" An older version of Claudine strode out of the café. She was taller, and her figure was thinner, but her hair was the same brunette shade as

Claudine's. The newcomer's expression was sharp with a hint of malice, but anyone looking at the two of them could tell they must be related.

"My cousin told me all about your shenanigans," the newcomer continued, scowling at them.

Maddie and Suzanne exchanged a wary look. Surely the woman couldn't be talking about … magic?

"What did you say to the mayor?" Claudine demanded.

"Nothing," Maddie replied, relief in her tone.

She was aware of curious glances directed their way from the couple of customers inside the café, and passersby on the sidewalk. But no one stopped to enquire what was going on, or to help them escape from Claudine and her cousin.

Not that they needed help. Maddie squared her shoulders, determined to be as polite as possible. Hopefully that would work in getting them out of here ASAP.

"Is this your cousin, Claudine?" Maddie smiled tentatively at the older woman.

"Yes. I'm Veronica," the woman said. "And Claudine's told me all about you two. How you used to work for her—" she sniffed "—until you quit and set up in opposition to her."

"It wasn't quite like that," Maddie said, then wondered if it actually was. She'd never thought of it in that light. She'd been miserable working for Claudine as a barista, and when Suzanne had suggested they start up their own business with a coffee truck, she'd been dubious at first. But Suzanne had been right to persist (or nag). Maddie had never been happier.

"There are a lot of people in this town who need coffee," Suzanne said. "We're providing a service."

"Just like I was yesterday." Claudine frowned. "I was providing an *iced coffee* service. Until you shut me down."

"The mayor said he'd received a complaint," Maddie put in. "And it wasn't us," she hastily added.

"We're going to find out who it was," Veronica said, her eyes narrowing. "And when we do – they better watch out!"

Maddie's eyes widened at the venom in the older woman's voice. She did not want to be on the receiving end of *that.*

"My cousin runs the best café in town," Veronica continued. "You girls better remember that."

"It's the only café in town," Suzanne snapped back, "and there are plenty of people who prefer our coffee to hers."

"Suzanne," Maddie hissed. She didn't want the confrontation to get worse, and she knew how Claudine and now apparently Claudine's cousin got under her bestie's skin.

"We won't delay you any longer," Maddie said in what she hoped was a conciliatory tone.

"Yeah!" Suzanne looked like she wanted to say more, but swallowed hard and strode down the street, not even checking to see if Maddie was with her.

Maddie smiled tightly at Claudine and Veronica, and hurried after her friend.

Once they reached the salad shop, Suzanne turned to Maddie. "I'm sorry,

Mads, I know I shouldn't have lost it back there, but that woman – oooh! I'm just sorry I didn't have a better comeback." Maddie was surprised that steam wasn't billowing out of Suzanne's ears.

"I know," Maddie replied, "but I think we should be careful. We don't want to rile Claudine any more, and now she has her cousin—"

"She seems even worse than Claudine." Suzanne wrinkled her nose. "I definitely wouldn't want to get on her bad side."

"You mean we aren't on her bad side already?"

Suzanne laughed, her sunny nature resurfacing. "Let's just try and forget about them – now that Claudine can't set up next to us, hopefully the whole thing will blow over by tomorrow."

**

That afternoon, one of their regular customers stopped by for an iced coffee.

"I've been meaning to try these," Pamela told them. Around fifty, she looked fit and trim, with short, layered sun-streaked hair.

"They're awesome," Suzanne enthused, taking their customer's money.

"Where's Trixie?" Pamela peered through the serving hatch.

"She's having a day at home." Maddie looked up from the machine with a smile. "I'll be sure to tell her you stopped by."

"You do that." Pamela smiled. "She's such a dear little thing. Seeing her when I come by for a coffee brightens my day. And I need some cheering up today, after seeing … *her*."

"Who?" Suzanne leaned forward to get the scoop.

"Veronica." Pamela wrinkled her nose, as if she could smell something rotten. "I nearly fainted when I saw her in town yesterday. And then she greeted me as cool as you please, when—" she shook her head, her mouth tightening.

"Milk and cream?" Maddie asked, sensing that the older woman might need some whipped cream therapy.

"Please." Pamela nodded.

Maddie made sure to put a healthy squirt of cream on the beverage, almost as much as Suzanne had put on hers yesterday.

"What happened?" Suzanne asked curiously. If she saw Maddie's frown, she ignored it.

"I know it's a long time ago but—" Pamela shook her head. "Some things you just don't get over. And I'm sure most people would think it's quite trivial in the scheme of things, but to me—" she sighed.

"Here you go." Maddie placed the iced coffee with its tall mound of whipped cream in front of Pamela, since Suzanne seemed too engrossed in the conversation to realize that Maddie had finished making the drink.

"Thank you." Pamela's face brightened as she plucked a straw from the dispenser.

"What happened?" Suzanne's eyes sparkled with curiosity.

"Maybe I shouldn't say anything." Pamela hesitated and took a sip of her beverage. "Mmm." Her eyes closed. "That is excellent, Maddie."

"Thank you," Maddie replied, pleased that she could make one of their customers happy for a second.

Pamela looked around the square as if checking for eavesdroppers, but she was the only person in the near vicinity.

She lowered her voice. "Veronica stole my place on the cheerleading squad – in high school."

"Oh." Suzanne looked a little disappointed at the revelation.

"I know." Pamela nodded. "You probably thought I was going to say something quite shocking. But it definitely upset me at the time – and when I allow myself to think about it, it still does."

"What did she do?" Maddie couldn't help herself. "It's okay, I shouldn't have asked," she said hastily.

"I don't mind telling you girls," Pamela replied, "as long as you keep it to yourselves."

"We will," they chorused. Suzanne mimed zipping her lips shut.

"It was a very small squad." Pamela took another sip of her drink. "Only four girls. The high school was smaller back then than it is now, so that's one of the reasons why we had a small cheerleading team. But it was considered prestigious back then to get a spot on the squad."

"I can imagine." Suzanne nodded, her ponytail swishing.

"I'd auditioned, and I'd done very well. I was a sophomore and the other three girls were a mix of juniors and seniors. There was only one spot available, and I'd created my own cheer to show them what I could do. The three cheerleaders told me there was only one person after me and to wait outside. All the other girls who had auditioned that afternoon had been told to go home. So I was hopeful that it meant that they'd chosen me, unless the person who auditioned after me was better."

"And the next girl was Veronica?" Suzanne guessed.

"Yep. I don't know how good she was, but she didn't play fair. Afterward, the head cheerleader came up to me and said they would have chosen me but they'd just found out I'd stolen the cheer I'd showed them." Pamela looked distressed. "That was a big deal back then. Heck, it still is."

"Veronica told them you'd auditioned with a stolen cheer?" Maddie couldn't believe it.

"Yep," Pamela said wryly. "They said they didn't condone that type of behavior and they'd never allow me on the team – ever. You have no idea how much I cried on the way home. It had been my dream to be on the cheerleading squad and that b–witch ruined it."

Maddie and Suzanne shared a sideways glance.

"You don't think she's really a witch, do you?" Suzanne asked.

"No." Pamela laughed without mirth. "I was trying to be polite." She took another sip of her iced concoction. "But that wasn't all. I was an outcast at school for the rest of the year. Someone blabbed about what had happened, and it wasn't me. So it was either the other cheerleaders or Veronica who told however many people that I'd auditioned with a stolen cheer. Apart from my best friend, everyone else treated me like a pariah."

"That's terrible." Suzanne looked shocked. "Do you think it was Veronica who tattled? After making it up in the first place?"

"But why would she do such an awful thing to you?" Maddie crinkled her brow, knowing Pamela didn't mean anything by her witch comment – she hoped. "Why you and none of the other girls?"

Pamela shrugged. "All I could think of at the time was the head girl must have told Veronica that it was between her and me, so she decided to play dirty."

"I'm sorry," Maddie said.

"Me too." Suzanne's ponytail bounced in sympathy.

"I can't believe she's come back to Estherville," Pamela continued. "When she left straight after high school, I think most of the town breathed a sigh of relief."

"Really?" Suzanne leaned forward.

"I wasn't the only person she sabotaged. She stole someone's boyfriend, and got another girl expelled from school."

"Wow," Maddie said softly.

"And I'm sure there's plenty more stuff like that she did back then, but none of her other victims spoke about it to anyone."

"We'd better stay out of her way then." Maddie shot Suzanne a speaking glance.

"Good idea, girls. Stay *far* away from her."

"It might be too late." Suzanne grimaced. "I think we're already on her radar."

"Then you better fly low, so she can't see you."

CHAPTER 3

The next morning, Luke stopped by the truck. Tall, with auburn hair and gorgeous green eyes, he made Maddie's heart race.

"Hi, Maddie." He smiled at her.

"Hi," Maddie replied breathlessly.

They'd just handled the morning rush and right now, he was their only customer.

Although she and Luke had been dating for a few months now, she still got blushy and flustered in his presence. Suzanne thought it was cute.

"That will be three-ninety, big brother." Suzanne held her hand out for the money. "If you want your usual regular latte."

"No health balls?" He scrutinized the counter.

"No." Suzanne sounded glum for an instant. "Some of our customers thought the weather was too hot for them. So we're serving iced coffee and lemon water instead."

Maddie had already set to work making her boyfriend's drink.

"We're still on for tonight, right, Maddie?" Luke handed his sister some cash.

"Yes." Maddie smiled at him, sure that everyone in the whole world could tell she was blushing right now.

"Mrrow!" Trixie waved a paw in his direction.

"How are you today, Trixie?" His lips twitched.

"Mrrow," she answered playfully.

Maddie was thankful that Trixie seemed to like Luke just as much as she did. She didn't know what she would have done if her familiar had disapproved of him.

Maddie handed Luke his drink, wishing she could take a peek at his future. But how could she, when he didn't even know she was a witch? Somehow, doing the Coffee Vision spell for her unknowing boyfriend seemed different to doing it for an unknowing customer. If she saw something good or bad on the surface of the coffee, she told them in a way that she hoped didn't raise suspicion that she had witchy abilities.

"What are you two doing tonight?" Suzanne asked, her face alive with curiosity.

"We're having dinner," Luke told his sister.

"At that little bistro in the next block," Maddie added.

"Ooh," Suzanne sounded wistful. "I wish I had a dinner date with someone."

"Why not ask Ramon?" Maddie suggested mischievously, immediately feeling guilty when Suzanne's face lit up, then fell.

"Ramon?" Luke enquired as only a big brother could.

"You know," Suzanne waved a hand in the direction of Ramon's salon at the other end of the square. "He's a masseur. And Spanish. And gorgeous."

"Isn't he a bit old for you?" Luke's eyes narrowed.

"Luke," Maddie whispered. She didn't want to get in the way of Suzanne and Luke's conversation, but she felt responsible for starting this topic in the first place.

Suzanne and Ramon had a flirty thing going on, but to Maddie's knowledge it had never progressed beyond that. She considered Ramon a friend, and thought Suzanne did too – although she did get dreamy-eyed over him.

"I'm twenty-seven, big brother. I think I'm old enough to date whoever I want." Suzanne firmed her lips as she looked pointedly at Luke.

"Okay, okay." Luke held up his hands in surrender. "But he better not take advantage of you, that's all I'm saying."

"Not much chance of that," Suzanne muttered.

Maddie's heart went out to her friend. It had been a few months since they'd met Ramon and although he seemed interested in Suzanne, he hadn't asked her out.

Luke chatted with them for a couple more minutes, then picked up his coffee and headed to his vehicle restoration workshop.

"I'm sorry I brought up Ramon." Maddie touched Suzanne's arm.

"It's okay." Suzanne summoned a wan smile. "You know how dreamy he is, and it's been fun flirting with him, but I guess I have to accept that's all it's going to be. And I'm okay with that. Really."

Maddie didn't know who her friend was trying to convince.

"Mrrow," Trixie sounded sympathetic.

"Thanks, Trixie." Suzanne stroked the cat. "I'll be fine. But maybe it's time I got out there more."

"Where?" Maddie poured an espresso shot, then turned it into a mocha by adding quality chocolate powder and steamed milk with a spectacular foam. "Here."

"Thanks." Suzanne took a sip and closed her eyes in enjoyment. "Why does chocolate make everything a little better?"

"Because it's awesome."

"Just like best friends." Suzanne smiled.

"Mrrow!"

Suzanne became serious. "I think it's time though, Mads. You and Luke are together, and I *love* that, because I'm sure we're going to be sisters one day, but if I want a special guy, I might have to do a little looking."

"You know I'll help you any way I can," Maddie said.

"Mrrow!" Trixie agreed.

"Thanks, you two." Suzanne beamed at Maddie and then Trixie.

"I know!" Grinding and hissing ensued as Maddie poured another shot. "Put that drink down and I'll make you another. And this time I'll do a Coffee Vision spell."

"Yes!" Suzanne plunked her cardboard cup down on the counter. "This is one of those times I'm glad we don't have any customers right now." She peered out of the serving hatch. "At least Claudine has gotten rid of her stand."

Maddie realized they'd been so busy that morning when they'd opened that she hadn't given Claudine's temporary iced coffee stall a thought.

"That's good news."

"Definitely."

Maddie finished making Suzanne's new mocha and focused on the cup, quieting her mind.

"Show me," Maddie whispered, brushing back her hair as she stared at the top layer of foam on the mocha. The foam swirled, then cleared.

"What do you see?" Suzanne tried to peer over her shoulder.

"Ramon."

"Really?" Suzanne looked hopeful, then her face fell. "That doesn't mean anything, though."

"He's talking to you," Maddie said.

"Anything else?" Suzanne asked eagerly.

"No." Maddie shook her head. "But it means you might see him in the next twenty-four hours."

"I guess." Suzanne picked up the cup and took a sip. "Yum." She blissfully closed her eyes, then sighed. "I wish I could make coffee like you do, Mads. Or else have—" she lowered her voice "—magical powers like you – and Trixie."

Maddie automatically looked around to check no one was listening. But the three of them were alone in the truck and there were no customers waiting to be served.

"You can do lots of things," Maddie pointed out. Sometimes she wished she were more like Suzanne, fearless and confident.

"But I don't think I'm super good at them, like you are with coffee."

"Well, we know I'm not super good with magic," Maddie murmured ruefully, still worried a passerby might overhear them.

"But you're getting better," Suzanne pointed out. "And Trixie is great at it."

"Mrrow." Trixie seemed to preen a little at the comment.

"But you're good at looking after our accounts," Maddie said, trying to cheer up her friend. It was unlike Suzanne to show self-doubt. "And if it was your idea that we go into business together."

"That's true." Suzanne brightened.

Maddie was so intent on their conversation that she didn't notice their new customer at first.

"Hello, Maddie, and Suzanne." A male with a deep, rich voice greeted them. His faint Spanish accent made everything he said sound enticing.

"Ramon." Maddie smiled.

"Hi." Suzanne also smiled but Maddie noticed she didn't bounce to the counter like she usually did when Ramon visited the truck.

"I have been hearing a lot about your iced coffees, Maddie," Ramon said, his gaze mostly focused on Suzanne. He was in his early forties and was tall, dark, and gorgeous. And single. He looked cool and comfortable in tailored chinos and a short-sleeved navy shirt.

"Then you should try one," Suzanne said, working the register. "Would you like cream on top?"

"No, I think not," Ramon replied, shifting slightly.

"Coming right up." Maddie gazed from her friend to Ramon and back again. Usually Suzanne and Ramon's flirty banter seemed to flow effortlessly. She knew her friend was disappointed that her flirtationship with the massage therapist hadn't evolved, but Ramon seemed a trifle ill at ease today. Or was it just her imagination?

"Mrrow," Trixie called, as if wanting Ramon to notice her.

"Ah, Trixie." He greeted the Persian. "And how are you today?"

"Mrrow," Trixie said coyly, waving a paw at him.

"That is good," he replied, a ghost of a smile on his lips.

"Here you go." Suzanne slid the icy cold caffeine in front of him.

Maddie noticed her friend was careful not to touch Ramon's fingers.

"Thank you." Ramon reached for a straw, then paused. "Suzanne, there is something I must ask you." His dark, liquid eyes captured her gaze. "I was thinking, perhaps we could go out to lunch sometime? When Maddie does not need you here."

Suzanne's expression brightened. For one unusual second she seemed lost for words.

"I'd like that," she said demurely.

"Then we must make a date." Ramon took his phone out of his pocket. "What about tomorrow?"

Suzanne looked at Maddie with a wide-eyed expression.

"Yes," Maddie said. "I'll be fine on my own."

"Excellent." Ramon pressed buttons on his phone. "I shall pick you up here at – twelve-thirty?"

Suzanne nodded, a dreamy expression on her face.

"Until then." He smiled at Suzanne, looking so handsome that Maddie had to suck in a breath. She just hoped Suzanne's legs were still able to hold her upright.

"I am *so* going to marry that man." Suzanne sank down on a stool and fanned herself.

Maddie noticed the rosy pink flush on her friend's cheeks.

"It looks like you mightn't have to go out searching for a special someone after all," she teased.

"I thought I was going to die when he asked me to lunch." Suzanne dramatically put a hand to her heart. "While at the same time, all I could think of was, *"Yes!"* and then, *"About time!"* She giggled.

"Mrrow!" Trixie put in.

"You'll be okay by yourself tomorrow, won't you, Mads?" Suzanne looked anxious for a second. "Maybe I should have said Saturday instead – or Sunday. But that's three whole days away!"

"I'll be fine," Maddie assured her friend. "Trixie can keep me company tomorrow. If you want to, Trix," she added to the cat.

"Mrrow!" Trixie seemed keen on the idea.

"What am I going to wear?" Suzanne's eyes widened. "I hope it's not going to be too hot tomorrow!"

"You'll have plenty of time tonight to decide," Maddie soothed her friend.

"You two will have to help me," Suzanne declared. "Right after we close up this afternoon."

"Mrrow!" Trixie agreed.

"Okay. But don't forget I'm having dinner with Luke tonight."

"Oh – yikes! Well, I'm sure we'll have plenty of time to choose an outfit before dinner," Suzanne said.

CHAPTER 4

It took two hours for Suzanne to decide what to wear for her lunch date with Ramon. Maddie had never seen her friend so indecisive. Finally, Suzanne chose a teal floaty dress, that looked cool and comfortable, as well as flattering her slim figure.

"Ramon is going to wonder why he never asked you out before now," Maddie told her friend, before hurrying home with Trixie to get ready for her own date.

"Did you have something to do with Ramon asking out Suzanne?" she asked her familiar as she quickly changed into a lilac dress.

"Mrrow." Trixie seemed affronted at the idea.

"I'm sorry," Maddie apologized as she brushed her hair. She met Trixie's turquoise gaze in the bedroom mirror. "I know you're not naughty with magic."

"Mrrow." Trixie sounded happier.

"I just wish I was a bit better at it," Maddie confided. "I think Suzanne and I worked out a while ago it's going to take me eight years to come into my full powers, if I keep on learning one new spell per full moon cycle." She put down the hairbrush. "I'll be thirty-five by then!"

"Mrrow," Trixie seemed to agree.

"Thanks." Maddie scrunched up her face.

Luke picked her up, and Trixie settled on the sofa, *Wytchcraft for the Chosen* out of sight.

Maddie enjoyed dinner with Luke, but wasn't sure whether to tell him about Suzanne having lunch with Ramon. In the end she decided it was up to her friend to tell Luke about it – if she wanted to.

After a meal of stuffed pork chops and chicken pot pie, finishing with a heavenly dessert of crème brulee, Luke took her home.

"Has Claudine been bothering you anymore?" he asked as she unlocked her front door.

"No. Thank goodness." She walked into the hall, keenly aware of him right behind her.

"The whole town seems to be talking about Veronica being back," he continued as they entered the kitchen.

"I wonder how long she's going to stay?" Maddie mused as she placed two mugs on the kitchen counter. They usually finished their dates with a latte and cuddling on the couch, before Luke departed.

"I don't think anyone wants her to visit any longer than necessary," he said, getting the milk out of the refrigerator for her.

She smiled her thanks, just as Trixie padded into the kitchen.

"Mrrow." She jumped on "her" kitchen chair and settled in, as if interested in their conversation.

"Suzanne and I heard something about Veronica doing something awful in high school." Maddie shuddered. "She doesn't sound like a nice person at all.

"What was it?" Luke asked curiously.

"I can't say," Maddie replied regretfully. "We promised not to mention it to anyone." She nibbled her lip. "I don't think I should have said anything."

"It's okay." Luke smoothed back a strand of her hair. "No one could accuse you of being a gossip."

Maddie smiled at him, once again appreciative that Luke just "got" her – apart from being a witch and Trixie being her familiar. At times she yearned to tell him – and at other times she was scared he wouldn't understand if she did.

She decided to shove that worrisome thought to the back of her mind, and just enjoy his company *right now*.

"Mrrow!" Trixie called. Apparently Maddie and Luke had spent too long gazing into each other's eyes.

Luke laughed, kissed Maddie on the forehead, then turned his attention to Trixie.

"What did you get up to today, Trixie?" he asked.

Trixie proceeded to tell him in cat, which involved a lot of "Mrrows", while Maddie finished making the coffee.

"Are you going to come to work with me tomorrow, Trix?" Maddie asked as she handed Luke his latte.

"Mrrow!" Trixie replied importantly, her turquoise gaze locking with

Maddie's. She instantly knew that Trixie wanted to know how Suzanne's lunch date would turn out with Ramon – if she didn't already somehow know in a psychic familiar sense!

"I think that's a yes." Luke grinned.

They chatted about their plans for the next couple of weeks, Luke suggesting they go out to dinner one night next week, and have a picnic at a local park on the weekend – cats weren't disallowed, so Trixie was also invited.

"You'll have to wear your harness," Maddie told her familiar.

"Mrrow," Trixie agreed, her eyes sparkling. Maddie knew the Persian liked being included in most of her activities.

After they spent a few minutes on the couch, Trixie demurely staying in the kitchen, Luke kissed Maddie goodbye and left.

Maddie sighed softly as she watched him get in his car. Dating Luke was a dream come true – she just hoped it would never end.

CHAPTER 5

The next morning, Suzanne's mind was not on her job of operating the register. She forgot orders, keyed in the wrong amounts, and even mixed up two of their favorite customers' names.

"Mrrow?" Trixie asked in concern during a lull.

"Yes." Maddie turned to Suzanne. "What Trixie said."

"Sorry, guys." Suzanne grimaced. "I don't know what's wrong with my head today. I just can't concentrate. All I can think about is having lunch with Ramon. And then I get a sick feeling in my stomach." She bit her lip. "Maybe I should cancel."

"No way." Maddie shook her head. "You know you want to have lunch with him."

"But I'm such a mess!" Suzanne wailed. "And that's not me."

"I know."

"Mrrow!"

Maddie studied her friend. She'd worn the outfit they'd chosen last night, the floaty teal dress, hidden at the moment behind a voluminous apron. Instead of her customary ponytail, her hair fell straight and shiny to just below her shoulders.

"My hair is driving me nuts." Suzanne shoved a strand of hair behind her ear. "I should have worn a ponytail like usual, and then brushed it out just before twelve-thirty."

"Mrrow." Trixie furrowed her furry brow, then scampered off the stool. She hooked her paw into a low drawer and pulled. Nosing in the drawer, she trotted over to Suzanne and bunted her hand.

"Thanks, Trixie." Suzanne smiled as she showed Maddie a hair elastic. "How did you know I had one in there?"

"Mrrow," Trixie said coyly, before jumping up on her stool.

"This feels so much better." Suzanne drew back her hair and twisted the band around her ponytail. "Now I'll be able to focus more."

Maddie hoped so, for their customers' sakes. But she was sure she'd been just as bad when going out with Luke for the first time. Even now, she couldn't stop smiling and blushing when she saw him.

Midmorning, they had a stream of customers. Suzanne was nearly back to her efficient self, only making a couple of minor errors.

"Hi girls." Amy, a middle-aged woman who worked at the small supermarket, greeted them.

"Your usual?" Suzanne asked with a smile.

"Please." She brought out her wallet.

Maddie started on a double cappuccino.

"I heard you had some trouble the other day," Amy continued, pushing back her wavy chestnut hair.

"You mean Claudine?" Suzanne frowned.

"Yeah. And her cousin Veronica." Amy shuddered.

"Do you know her?" Maddie asked curiously as she sprinkled a generous amount of chocolate powder on top of the foam.

"Unfortunately." Amy grimaced. "That woman is bad news. You girls should stay away from her."

"We plan to." Suzanne's ponytail bounced.

"Mrrow!"

"That's good." Amy nodded in approval, reserving a smile for Trixie. "I definitely need my coffee today. A new guy has started as acting manager since Mr. Jenkins is away on an extended vacation. He's younger than me, but seems to like bossing me around." She scowled.

"But you've been working there for years," Suzanne exclaimed. "Why didn't they make you acting manager?"

"I applied, but didn't get it because I don't have a college degree." Amy took a big sip of her coffee, as if hoping that would make things better.

"That's terrible!"

Maddie nodded in agreement.

"Mrrow," Trixie murmured.

"And it's all that – that – *Veronica's* fault." Amy cast a glance at Trixie. "I don't want to swear in front of sweet Trixie."

"That's very thoughtful," Maddie replied.

"I had a decent chance of going to college," Amy continued, as if she couldn't hold her grievance in any longer. "I was always a good student, and I was in the running for a scholarship that would pay for practically everything. But Mom got sick in my senior year and some of the time I should have been studying I spent looking after her instead. Not that I resented her for it," she added hastily.

"That must have been tough," Maddie murmured.

"It was." Amy took a fortifying sip. "My grades slipped, and I didn't know what to do. Then Veronica suggested I …" she hesitated. "Oh heck, everyone knew about it at the time, anyway. She suggested I break into the principal's office and get the answers to the final exam. If I could ace it, I could probably still win the scholarship. So I did." She lifted the cardboard cup to her lips.

"What happened?" Suzanne asked, her eyes wide.

Maddie noticed that even Trixie was leaning forward, intent on Amy's next words.

"I got caught." Amy closed her eyes in remembered regret. "And I was expelled. There went my scholarship, and there went college. It was on my permanent record. Even if I could manage to get student loans or a work-study program, what sort of college would accept a cheater?"

"But … how did you get caught?" Suzanne crinkled her brow. That question had been on the tip of Maddie's tongue as well.

"Veronica." Amy's expression darkened. "She was the only one who knew what I was planning to do. It had even been her idea! And guess what? She got the scholarship I'd applied for."

"Goodness!" Maddie stared at Amy. "That's – that's—"

"Diabolical? Fiendish? Take your pick," Amy said bitterly. "And her scheming ruined my life – or I allowed it to. I got my GED, but I couldn't face applying to colleges, throwing myself on their mercy, and getting turned down. My family couldn't afford to pay for college, which might have been one way to get in, if there was a university that wasn't so fussy about their applicants.

"So here I am, fifty, and being bossed around by a kid half my age, because he has a college degree and I don't."

"I'm so sorry," Maddie replied.

"Mrrow," Trixie added softly.

"So stay away from Veronica. If she wants something you have, I think she'll do whatever it takes to snatch it from you."

With that piece of advice, Amy headed across the square to the supermarket.

"Wow." Suzanne sank down on a stool. "I can't believe that."

"I know." Maddie flopped on her own stool. "Poor Amy."

"Make sure I remember this if we have another run in with Claudine – and Veronica."

"We better not," Maddie said with feeling.

"Mrrow!"

The two girls turned to look at the Persian, who looked definite in her agreement.

"I think we should take Trixie's advice," Maddie said.

"Deal." Suzanne's ponytail bobbed.

A couple more customers stopped by, then Suzanne checked her watch, shrieking.

"It's twelve-twenty, Mads. Why didn't you tell me?"

"I didn't know," Maddie replied truthfully. The lunch crowd had been slower than usual today, which was why she hadn't realized it was nearing the time of Suzanne's lunch date with Ramon. "Sorry."

"I've got to fix my hair!" Suzanne pulled out a compact from her purse and unfastened her ponytail. She grabbed a comb and yanked. "Ow!"

"Slow down," Maddie told her, manning the register as a customer approached, asking for an iced coffee.

"Thank goodness it's not hot today," Suzanne continued. "Trix, how does my hair look?" She bent down slightly.

"Mrrow," Trixie sounded approving.

"Thanks!"

"Apron." Maddie pulled an espresso shot.

"Oh, yeah!" Suzanne yanked off the brown smock and smoothed down her dress. She placed a hand on her chest. "I think I need to sit for a second."

"Mrrow?" Trixie patted her mouth area as she stared at Suzanne.

"What is it, Trix?" Suzanne knitted her brow as she peered at the cat. "What are you trying to tell me?"

"Mrrow!" Trixie patted her mouth again, this time more urgently.

Maddie stifled a giggle, glad the iced coffee customer had just wondered off, slurping his drink.

"I think she's asking if you want to put on some lip-gloss," Maddie told her friend.

"Eeek!" Suzanne jumped off the stool, as if stung by a wasp. "How could I have forgotten?" She rummaged through her purse, her hand shaking as she colored her mouth. "Thanks, Trix," she mumbled through her half open lips.

Putting away the gloss, Suzanne sank on the stool again. "Maybe I should cancel, Mads. I feel really weird. Like I'm going to be sick. Maybe I've caught a virus or something. I should just go home and rest."

"You'll be fine," Maddie said bracingly. "It's just nerves, that's all. Isn't that what you said to me when I started dating Luke?"

"But that was different." Suzanne frowned. "I *never* feel like this."

"I think it just means you really like Ramon."

"Yeah." A dreamy smile passed over Suzanne's face. "I do."

"You do what?" A faint Spanish male accent.

"Ramon!" Suzanne jumped up. "Hi!"

"I am sorry I am a couple of minutes late," he said, looking gorgeous in tailored slacks and a long-sleeved cream shirt.

"I didn't even notice." Suzanne beamed at him.

Maddie noticed Ramon's eyes flared a little as he took in Suzanne. She looked cool and collected in her floaty dress, her straight, shiny hair out of its customary ponytail. Nobody would have guessed she'd been a nervous wreck two minutes ago.

"Shall we?" He held out his arm.

Suzanne exited the truck and took his arm, casting a smiling glance over her shoulder at Maddie and Trixie as she embarked on her date.

"That leaves the two of us to handle the rest of the lunch crowd," Maddie informed Trixie.

"Mrrow!" Trixie looked confident as she settled back on her stool.

Since business was down a little, Maddie was able to handle the customers solo, only wishing for Suzanne's presence a couple of times. All the while she was making lattes and iced coffees, she wondered how Suzanne's date was faring. She just hoped her best friend was having an incredible time.

***

"Hi."

Maddie looked up from her sandwich to find Luke standing at the counter.

"Hi." She put down her lunch and rushed to the counter, wishing she could bounce like Suzanne.

There had been a lull around one-thirty, and she'd taken the opportunity to eat her sandwich.

"Mrrow," Trixie greeted Luke.

"Hi Trixie." He grinned at the Persian. "Still on for our picnic on the weekend?"

"Mrrow!" Trixie purred.

"It's so cute that you talk to her like that," Maddie said, unable to stop a smile blossoming over her face.

"I think I picked it up from you." He chuckled.

Maddie realized with a start she did speak to Trixie like a person – or a creature who could understand everything she said. But she had the advantage of knowing that Trixie wasn't an ordinary cat – she was a familiar – *her* familiar.

"Where's Suzanne?" Luke peered into the truck.

"She's at lunch," Maddie said, suddenly having an *uh-oh* moment. Now she wished she'd told Luke last night about Suzanne's date with Ramon – but would Suzanne have wanted her to? Not that there was anything to worry about. Ramon was a nice guy – as well as being super hot and having a sexy Spanish accent. But Maddie knew if Luke and Ramon stood side by side, she would pick Luke every time.

"Don't you usually have lunch together?" he asked curiously.

"Yes." She hesitated.

"What is it?" Luke looked concerned. "Is Suzanne okay?"

"She's having lunch with Ramon." It came out in a rush. She could not lie to him.

"What?" He frowned.

"They're having lunch." She turned to Trixie, a *help me out here* look on her face.

"Mrrow." Trixie seemed to nod her head.

"I don't think Trixie has a problem with it." Maddie attempted to lighten the moment.

Luke cracked a reluctant smile as he looked at the Persian, who suddenly wore a very cute and appealing expression.

"Well, if Trixie thinks it's okay ..." He shook his head. "What am I doing?"

"Hoping your sister enjoys her lunch," Maddie told him. "That's all." She moved over to the machine. "Maybe you need a latte – with hazelnut syrup."

He nodded.

"And this one's on the house." She waved away his offer to pay.

"Why didn't you tell me about Suzanne and … Ramon?"

"I wasn't sure how you'd react," she told him, pulling a shot. "Besides, Suzanne's my best friend. I don't want to hide anything from you—" *like being a witch* "—but I don't want to get in the middle of you and Suzanne either."

"I can understand that." He nodded thoughtfully. "I just don't want my sister to get hurt."

"Neither do I." They gazed at each other in understanding.

Luke stayed for a little while, praising the hazelnut latte. When he departed, Maddie let out a sigh of relief. She was glad he understood the position she was in with regard to his sister's love life. Now all she needed was Suzanne's new romance to run smoothly.

CHAPTER 6

Suzanne came back from lunch just after two-thirty.

"I had the best time, Mads," she gushed, her blue eyes sparkling. "We went to that little bistro you and Luke visited. Oh, it was divine! We had red wine and beef olives, and dessert was raspberry panna cotta. And we talked."

"That's wonderful." Maddie smiled at her friend.

"Mrrow!" Trixie seemed to agree.

"Oh, Trixie, Ramon is just the best." Suzanne blushed, a big grin on her face. Then she sobered. "You don't think – Trix, you wouldn't be able to tell me, would you – oh, I'm being silly." She looked embarrassed.

"What is it?" Maddie peeked through the serving hatch. No customers. In fact, nobody in sight.

"Ramon seems – I don't know." She sighed. "Too perfect. He's never been married. I mean, are the women mad in Spain? He's been in the US for a while, but why wasn't he snapped up in Spain?

He's gorgeous, and interesting, and well mannered, and—"

"Stop." Maddie held up her hand. "I'm sure there's nothing wrong with Ramon." She hadn't received the slightest whisper of intuition that there had been anything "off" with the Spaniard. These days, a thirteen-year difference or so between a couple seemed to be common. The most important thing was that Ramon was a good guy who treated Suzanne well.

"Trixie?" Suzanne turned to the Persian.

"You don't believe me?" Maddie asked.

"It's not that, Mads." Suzanne looked discomfited. "You know I totally believe in your witchy powers and always have, ever since we met in middle school."

"When I could only do the Coffee Vision spell," Maddie said ruefully.

"I always wished I could do something cool like that," Suzanne replied with a smile. "I just thought maybe Trixie could give me a second opinion – on Ramon."

"Okay," Maddie said. "But what if Trixie disagrees with me? Whose opinion will you prefer?"

"I'm hoping she's going to say the same thing you are," Suzanne said.

"Mrrow!" Trixie seemed to agree.

"Was that a yes, Trix?" Suzanne scrutinized the cat. "Do you agree with Maddie? That I'm just being silly and there's nothing wrong with Ramon?" She held her breath.

"Mrrow!" Trixie said definitively, appearing to nod her head.

"Phew!" Suzanne let out a whoosh of relief.

"See?" Maddie said, secretly glad that her familiar had in fact agreed with her.

"I'm sorry I doubted you, Mads." Suzanne gave her a hug. "But oh, I've never felt like this before. My feelings have been building ever since we met him, and now that he stops by a few times per week at the truck, plus the massages, I don't know … I'm really smitten!"

"I'm happy for you," Maddie said, smiling.

"Mrrow!" Trixie added.

"Thanks, you two. I just hope he feels the same about me."

"He asked you out, didn't he?" Maddie said. It wasn't like her bestie to show self-doubt.

"Yes, but what if he realizes it was a mistake?"

"Did he seem to have a good time?"

"Yes." Suzanne blushed.

"I don't think he would have asked you out if he thought it would only be a one time date," Maddie said, feeling her way. She wasn't the most experienced dater, that was for sure. "Because it would be a bit awkward for you two if he came by the truck again for a coffee, wouldn't it?"

"Yeah." Suzanne nodded. "That's what I've been thinking, all last night and this morning. I guess that's one of the reasons why I was so nervous getting ready today."

"You were? I hadn't noticed," Maddie teased.

Suzanne punched her lightly on the arm.

Before they could continue their bantering, clanging sounded from near the truck. Maddie and Suzanne looked at each other.

"Oh no!" Suzanne peered out of the serving hatch. "It's Veronica!"

"Let me see!" Maddie joined her at the counter.

Veronica was assembling the same collapsible table Claudine had used the other day.

"She's not allowed to do that!" Suzanne glowered.

"Then we better tell her – I guess," Maddie said, not wanting to have another confrontation with the woman.

"You bet we will." Suzanne wrenched open the rear door of the truck and marched out.

"Mrrow?" Trixie furrowed her brow at Suzanne departing.

"Stay here, Trix," Maddie said. "We'll be back in a minute."

Trixie sighed and stayed on the stool.

"You can't do that!" Maddie heard Suzanne's raised voice.

"Uh oh." Maddie grimaced at Trixie and jumped out of the truck. She knew Claudine rubbed her friend the wrong way – she just hoped Veronica's presence didn't make matters even worse.

"Yes, I can." Veronica stood, feet apart, hands on her hips. Her table was erected right next to Brewed from the Bean.

"Do you have permission?" Maddie asked politely, joining them.

Veronica scowled. "I don't need permission. It's a free country. I can do whatever I like."

"Not in the town square you can't," Suzanne informed her. She reached into her pocket. "Why don't I call the mayor and ask him if you're allowed to set up here?"

Veronica's eyes narrowed. "What he doesn't know won't hurt him."

"But you don't have a problem hurting our business?" Maddie asked.

"Like I said, I can do whatever I want, coffee girl." Veronica's scowl deepened. "You might have run off Claudine the other day but I don't scare so easily. Since everyone's buying iced coffee from you, setting up here is an ideal location. And I'm going to keep the profits."

Suzanne snorted. "Good luck making any if your cousin made the coffee."

"What's that supposed to mean?" Veronica demanded.

"Just that there's a reason everyone comes to *us* for their coffee," Suzanne told her.

"Because you've badmouthed Claudine to everyone," Veronica returned.

"We have not!" Maddie drew herself up to her full height of five foot five. She didn't like Claudine, or her coffee, but she didn't think she'd ever said a negative thing about the other woman's coffee to anyone – apart from Suzanne – and Trixie. And maybe Luke. But no one else.

"Broomf!" Trixie peered out of the serving hatch. She looked very cross.

"I don't know how you're allowed to have a cat inside a food prep area," Veronica continued. "Maybe I should complain to the mayor about that!"

"We have permission," Suzanne said loftily. "In fact, the mayor is one of Trixie's favorite customers."

"Is everything okay, girls?" A woman in her early fifties hurried over to them. "Are you closing early today? I thought I'd try one of your iced coffees – oh!" The woman stood stock still as she caught a glimpse of Veronica.

"Look who it is! Grace." A smirk snaked around Veronica's lips.

The woman called Grace flushed slightly, but stood her ground.

"Veronica. I'd heard you were back."

"Not for good, though. Because who would want to live *here*?" Veronica replied. "Just visiting Claudine and seeing what I can do to help her."

"Let me make you a coffee." Maddie gently touched Grace's arm. She looked a little upset.

"I'm calling the mayor right now." Suzanne pressed some buttons on her phone.

Grace followed Maddie back to the truck.

"Veronica! What are you doing?" Claudine's nasal screech stopped them in their tracks. Claudine rushed over to Veronica. "I told you not to set up here!"

"You can't tell me what to do, little cousin."

"Yes, I can." Now it was Claudine's turn to put her hands on her hips as she glared at Veronica. "Take that table down right now! You can help me in the shop."

She stalked off to her café, ignoring everyone else.

Maddie continued to her truck, not wanting to make eye contact with Veronica. She tapped Suzanne on the arm and gestured toward Trixie still peering out of the serving hatch.

"Come on," she murmured to her friend.

Grace followed them to Brewed from the Bean, seemingly escaping Veronica as well.

"I can't believe I've run into *her*," Grace said, standing on the customer side of the counter.

"Do you know her?" Suzanne asked curiously.

"Suzanne!" Maddie hissed.

"I did – sort of." Grace sighed. "I think you'd better put a double shot of espresso in my iced coffee, Maddie."

"Of course." Maddie set to work, grinding and hissing ensuing from the machine.

"Mrrow?" Trixie had left the serving hatch and had settled back on her stool. She looked enquiringly at Grace.

"You are such a sweet thing, Trixie," she told the Persian.

"Mrrow." Trixie sounded as if she said, "*Yes, I know.*"

"I don't really want to talk about it, girls. It happened a long time ago." Grace sounded sad.

"We understand," Maddie said, sending Suzanne a warning glance.

"Yes," Suzanne added, a tad reluctantly.

"All I'll say is that she stole the man I was in love with. And I've never met anyone else."

CHAPTER 7

"I can't believe Veronica has riled so many people," Suzanne said, slurping on an iced coffee. It was almost four o'clock – closing time – and there weren't any customers.

"I know," Maddie said, adding some chocolate powder to her icy concoction. If it worked, she'd add it to the menu tomorrow.

"Mrrow!" Trixie said in agreement.

"I'm just glad we didn't go to school with Veronica," Maddie commented. She closed her eyes and took a sip of her icy mocha. Mmm. "But let's not talk about her anymore today." She opened her eyes and grinned at Suzanne. "I've just made an iced mocha and I think it's good enough to put on the menu."

"If you say it's good, then it must be awesome," Suzanne teased. "You can be very critical of your own barista skills."

"Mrrow," Trixie added knowingly.

"See what you think." Maddie stuck another straw in her cup and offered it to Suzanne.

"OMG." Suzanne's eyes widened. "That is *good*."

"Mrrow?" Trixie looked toward the icy cup.

"Chocolate is bad for cats, Trix," Maddie said regretfully. "So is coffee."

"Broomf!" Trixie's mouth settled into a pout.

"I know what will cheer Trixie up," Suzanne said to Maddie. "When's the next full moon? I'll definitely be over at your house to see what new spell you'll be able to do."

Maddie looked at the small calendar on the truck wall. "It's in two days."

"Awesome." Suzanne looked excited. "Do you think Maddie will learn a new spell then, Trix?"

"Mrrow," Trixie said, which sounded like, *"Of course, with me helping her."*

"Keep your voice down," Maddie muttered, a little uneasy about how much they were talking about magic in public – even if they were in the van and there was no one meandering about outside.

"You know I'm careful," Suzanne told her.

"I know. Sorry. I think Veronica being here and everyone seeming to have a problem with her in the past has put me a little on edge."

"It's strange how many people she betrayed years ago, isn't it?" Suzanne mused. "Why would she want to come back?"

"Perhaps she thought people had forgotten about what she did," Maddie replied.

"Instead they seemed to have remembered better than ever."

"Mrrow!"

***

The next morning, Maddie arrived at work with Trixie. The first thing she did after setting up was to write *Iced Mochas* on the little blackboard they kept for their specials.

"Hi," Suzanne arrived, out of breath. "Sorry I'm late."

"Only by three minutes," Maddie teased. "Look!" She gestured to the blackboard set up on the counter.

"Cool!" Suzanne grinned. "Hopefully this will attract more customers, since business was down a little yesterday."

"Maybe it was just one of those days," Maddie said.

"Or maybe Veronica's been bad mouthing your coffee."

"What?" Maddie stared at her friend. "Mrrow?"

Suzanne shrugged. "It's just a theory I came up with last night to explain yesterday's sales – or lack of them."

"You mean you weren't dreaming about Ramon?" Maddie teased gently.

"Yeah." Suzanne didn't even have to think about it. "But anyway, I'm going over to Claudine's café and see if there's anything funny going on."

"No, you're not." Maddie shook her head. "The less we have to do with Claudine and Veronica, the better. Even if they are saying untrue things about our coffee, confronting them isn't going to work. They'll probably deny it. And," Maddie said, taking a breath to continue, "all our customers know what our coffee is like. So I think we should just chalk up yesterday's slow sales as one of those blips we occasionally get."

"You're right." Suzanne sighed. "Maybe I'm just trying to take my mind off the fact that I haven't heard from Ramon since our lunch date."

"Oh." Maddie didn't know what to think. "But that was only yesterday. He could be busy with clients, just like we've been busy here."

"That's what I've been telling myself." She shook her head, her ponytail jiggling. "I've decided I'm just going with the flow, and not stressing about it. If he calls, fine. If he doesn't, fine." Her eyes suddenly lit up. "Maybe Trixie could help me with a love potion." Then her shoulders sagged. "That's wrong, isn't it?"

"Yes!"

Maddie waited for Trixie to chime in. When she didn't, Maddie looked at her familiar enquiringly.

"Mrrow," Trixie sounded a little reluctant to agree.

"I noticed you didn't ask me to help you with a—" she cast a glance through the serving hatch but there was no one around, not even an early morning jogger "—love potion."

"That's because you don't know how to do one," Suzanne told her. "But I thought Trixie might."

"Well, that's honest." Maddie saw the funny side and stifled a reluctant giggle.

A sudden influx of exercisers asking for water and the occasional latte kept them busy and chit chat to a minimum. After the early morning crowd, employees needing a shot of caffeine on the way to work kept Maddie and Suzanne occupied until a welcome lull around nine o'clock.

Suzanne sighed as she stared out at the now empty town square. "I wonder when I'll see him again."

Maddie guessed she was talking about Ramon.

"Why don't you pop by his salon?" she suggested. "You could always book another massage with him."

"I could, couldn't I?" Suzanne brightened, then hesitated. "But that won't make me look … desperate, will it?"

"How many times has he stopped by here for coffee?" Maddie posed the question.

"A lot." Suzanne smiled, then her mouth pulled down. "But everyone knows if you want a good caffeine experience they need to come here – unless they're awesome at making it themselves at home."

"Which I think Ramon is," Maddie replied. The Spaniard's knowledge of coffee kept Maddie on her toes to make him the best coffee every time – something she endeavored to do for all her customers, even the ones she'd seen patronizing Claudine's café.

"So …" Suzanne said slowly.

"So, there must be a reason he comes by so often, and it's probably not to help support Brewed from the Bean."

"You think?" Suzanne brightened. "Maybe I will stop by his salon at lunch – if you can spare me."

"Of course." Maddie nodded.

"Mrrow," Trixie agreed.

"But …" Maddie smiled. "I don't think you'll need to." She glanced at the serving hatch.

A tall, dark-haired man strode up to the counter.

"Hello, Suzanne." A faint Spanish accent.

"Ramon." Suzanne smiled as she walked sedately – not bounced – to the counter.

Maddie wondered at it, but her friend looked happy to see him.

"I am sorry I have not been in touch," he told her, "but I have not had a moment to myself."

"I understand." Suzanne nodded.

Maddie busied herself at the machine, not that she had any orders to fill. But she didn't want either of them to think she was eavesdropping, although it was practically impossible *not* to hear their conversation.

"I enjoyed our lunch very much," Ramon continued. "Perhaps we could do it again – on Saturday?"

"I'd like that." Suzanne's ponytail bounced.

"I shall look forward to it." He smiled. "What time do you finish here on Saturday? I shall come for you."

"One o'clock."

"Then I will be here," he promised.

After he left, Maddie realized he hadn't said hello to her or Trixie as he usually did. He'd only had eyes for Suzanne.

"Eeek!" Suzanne spun around, a grin on her face. "I'm seeing him again!"

"Mrrow!" Trixie sounded approving.

"I wasn't trying to," Maddie said, "but I couldn't help overhearing. I'm so happy for you!"

"We'll both have dates on the weekend!" Suzanne looked excited. "Me with Ramon and you and Luke on your picnic."

"And Trixie," Maddie added.

"Mrrow!" Trixie chimed in.

"Sorry, Trix," Suzanne apologized.

"I'll make sure we close up by one o'clock on Saturday," Maddie pledged.

"Awesome!" Suzanne high-fived her.

The rest of the morning passed without any more excitement. And, to Maddie's relief, no sign of Claudine or her cousin Veronica.

At lunchtime, Suzanne stifled a yawn.

"Up late last night?" Maddie teased.

"I couldn't sleep," she admitted. "I was too busy thinking about Ramon. Maybe I should buy one of those power salads for lunch for an energy boost."

"Good idea," Maddie said. She hadn't heard her alarm that morning, and Trixie had slept in a little as well, which meant she hadn't had time to make a sandwich for lunch.

She looked out at the town square. No customers lining up for a lunchtime caffeine fix.

"Why don't we go now?"

"Mrrow!" Trixie hopped off her stool, pawed open a drawer, and picked out a turquoise harness.

"Yes." Maddie smiled as she took the harness from her familiar. "You can come with us, Trix."

Once she'd buckled the harness on the Persian, the three of them left the truck and headed to the other side of the square to the salad shop.

"The only thing I hate is having to walk past Claudine's café," Suzanne grumbled.

"Me too."

"Mrrow." Trixie pulled on the harness, directing them to a small laneway near the coffee shop.

"You want us to go this way?" Maddie peered into the gloomy alley. She'd walked down it a few times when she worked for Claudine, but hadn't ventured down it for a while.

"Mrrow." Trixie pulled again on the harness.

"This goes around to the rear of Claudine's café. That means she can't confront us like she did the other day when we walked past," Suzanne mused. "Why don't we try it?"

"Mrrow!" Trixie agreed.

"All right."

The trio walked down the laneway, then turned right at the end. Another lane – this one more like an alley – allowed them to walk behind Claudine's café. There were trash cans lined up in a row, all looking very tidy – the lids on properly, and no mess on the ground, either. Maddie was impressed at Claudine's neatness. When she'd worked for the woman, she hadn't had to deal with the garbage much – at the time, Claudine had taken care of it.

All tidy except for the last trash can. The lid was slightly ajar, and black hair like strands were strewn over the rim of the can.

"That's weird." Suzanne stopped and stared at the anomaly.

Intuition suddenly hit Maddie as her friend took a step toward the trash can.

"I don't think we should touch it," Maddie said.

Trixie pulled on the harness toward the can.

"No, Trixie." Maddie and her familiar shared a knowing glance. "I think we should leave this to …" She couldn't think of who they should call. The sheriff? Claudine?

"What are you two talking about?" Suzanne lifted the lid – and screamed.

Veronica's dead face stared back at them.

CHAPTER 8

One hour later, Maddie, Trixie and Suzanne sat on stools in their coffee truck.

"Why didn't you tell me not to look inside that can?" Suzanne grumbled, sipping on a double latte.

"I think I did," Maddie said mildly, sticking a straw in a desperately needed iced mocha.

"Mrrow," Trixie agreed.

Once Suzanne had finished screaming, she'd run a few steps down the alley before realizing she'd left Maddie and Trixie behind. They got out of there as fast as possible, Maddie dialing the sheriff's office as they ran to the apparent safety of the town square.

Maddie hadn't been sure whether they should have entered the café instead and broken the bad news to Claudine, but she thought a law enforcement officer would be more skilled at it.

After being told to stay at their coffee truck, Maddie and Suzanne watched a sheriff's vehicle arrive at the café.

Maddie had tried to keep her mind on making beverages for their customers. Suzanne, too, seemed to have difficulty ringing up the correct orders.

"I wonder if Detective Edgewater will be in charge of the investigation," Suzanne pondered, after taking a big gulp of her latte.

"I hope so," Maddie replied. So far, he had been the only detective they'd dealt with, apart from his nephew Detective Rawson, when Maddie had taken part in a big barista competition where one of the judges had been murdered.

"Maybe you'd better get a vanilla cappuccino ready for him, just in case," Suzanne suggested.

"Good idea." One taste of Maddie's cappuccino, and the detective had been hooked.

"Speak of the …" Suzanne took another hit of her latte.

A portly man in his sixties, with gray hair more salt than pepper, approached the truck. He was dressed in plain clothes – a worn brown suit with a white shirt, and navy tie slightly askew at the neck.

"I can't believe you two found a dead body – again," he greeted them.

"I know," Suzanne said glumly. "And I was the one to find her – Veronica." She shuddered, then gulped down her latte.

"I'm sorry," he replied, whipping out an old-fashioned notebook that peeked out of the top pocket of his suit jacket. "What were you two doing in that alley?" He looked disapproving.

"Vanilla cappuccino?" Maddie asked hopefully, trying to direct his attention away from their earlier activities.

"Mrrow," Trixie added, as if she approved of the idea.

"Hello, Trixie." His face broke into a reluctant smile.

"Mrrow," Trixie replied in greeting, sitting up straight on her stool.

"Okay, a vanilla cappuccino sounds good." He handed some cash to Suzanne.

Maddie focused on making his coffee as he started asking them questions.

"Why were you behind Claudine's café?" he asked, his pencil at the ready to jot down their answers.

"We were going to the salad shop," Suzanne replied.

"And you went that way?" His eyebrow flickered.

"We didn't want to run into Claudine," Maddie said, handing him his beverage.

"We thought if we walked past her front entrance, she might accost us, like she did the other day." Suzanne frowned.

"Ah." He wrote down something. "And why did she confront you then?"

"Because she'd set up a stand next to us," Suzanne answered. "Which she's not supposed to do."

"Mrrow!" Trixie added.

"And she upset Trixie," Maddie said, feeling a little guilty at doing so. She wondered if Detective Edgewater was susceptible to Trixie's feelings, like the mayor had been.

"I'd heard about that." He nodded. "Okay, so why did you dig around in her trash cans?"

"We didn't!" Suzanne's voice was indignant. "The lid was out of place compared to the other cans all lined up, so I peeked inside because I was curious." She grimaced and sank down on her stool.

"And then we called the sheriff's department," Maddie added.

"How did she ... die?" Suzanne asked.

"It looks like she was hit over the head with a heavy object," he replied. "We won't know more until after the autopsy."

"Oh." Suzanne looked like she was sorry she'd asked.

"Did you know the victim—" he looked at a page in his notebook "— Veronica Darin?"

"No."

"Not really."

"Which is it?" he asked.

"We didn't really know her," Maddie said, "but we'd spoken to her a couple of times."

"What did you think about her?" he asked curiously.

"I don't think you want to know," Suzanne told him.

"Mrrow!"

"I don't think Trixie liked her, either," Maddie said.

"And she's a pretty good judge of character," Suzanne added loyally.

"Mrrow." Trixie looked pleased at the praise.

The detective's mouth edged up in a smile.

"Do you know anyone else who had a run in with the victim?"

"Claudine," Suzanne answered instantly.

"Suzanne!" Maddie hissed.

"Well, she did," Suzanne replied. "Veronica was setting up her *illegal* iced coffee stand yesterday and Claudine rushed over and screeched at her to pull it down."

"Is that so?" he asked thoughtfully.

"We were out there too," Maddie felt dutybound to say. "We'd just told her that she needed to have permission to put up a stand here, and that's when Claudine told her to take it down."

"Anyone else have a grudge against her, as far as you know?" he continued.

"We've heard some things," Maddie said cautiously. "She didn't sound like a nice person when she lived here a long time ago."

"Apparently she went to high school here," Suzanne commented.

"Yes." Detective Edgewater nodded. "Anything else?"

Maddie and Suzanne looked at each other indecisively.

"W-e-l-l," Suzanne started. "I think she did some awful things to the other students at high school," Suzanne said.

"That was a long time ago." Detective Edgewater frowned. "Thirty-two years, give or take."

"Yes."

He sighed and put his notebook away. Then he picked up his cappuccino and took a sip.

"Excellent as usual, Maddie." He smiled briefly. "Now, if you hear anything about this matter, let me know. But that's all. Let the sheriff's department deal with it. And we will."

"Okay." Suzanne nodded.

"Yes," Maddie agreed.

Trixie didn't say anything, she just sat demurely on her stool.

"Hmm." The detective didn't look convinced. He took another sip of his drink, then departed.

A loud growling sound made Maddie freeze.

"What's that?" she frowned.

"My stomach." Suzanne looked embarrassed as she held a hand to her tummy. "I'm starving. We missed lunch because of what happened. I can't believe I'm hungry after seeing … Veronica, but I am."

"Why don't we go get something to eat?"

"Do you think the salad shop will deliver? I really don't want to go near Claudine's café again today."

"Good thinking." Maddie nodded.

Suzanne fished out her phone and dialed the salad shop.

"Yes!" She snapped her fingers. "Two power salads coming right up!"

Maddie and Suzanne exchanged grins, before suddenly becoming swamped by a deluge of customers, all talking about the murder.

Everyone seemed to think it was *terrible* that *another* murder had been committed in sleepy Estherville, but none of them seemed sorry Veronica was dead.

"Maybe the whole town was in on it," Suzanne whispered out of the side of her mouth as their last customer departed.

"I know." Maddie nodded, *her* stomach now grumbling. She checked her watch. "How long ago did you order the salads?"

"Sorry it took so long. Everyone came into the shop at once, talking about the murder." A teenage delivery boy rushed up to the truck. "Two power salads and two quinoa coconut cacao cookies."

"Thanks." Suzanne handed him some cash.

He waved to Trixie, a big grin on his face as he spied her, then hurried back across the square.

"Quinoa coconut cacao cookies?" Maddie crinkled her brow.

"I figured we deserved a treat, and the shop only has healthy stuff." Suzanne opened her brown paper bag, plucking out a cookie and biting into it. "Mmm." She closed her eyes as she savored the bite. "Not bad for healthy stuff."

"Mrrow?" Trixie asked.

"Do you want some lunch, Trix?" Maddie pulled open a drawer and grabbed a bag of dry food, shaking brown crunchy pellets into a bowl for her familiar.

"Mrrow!" Trixie investigated the bowl and started crunching.

Maddie opened her container and forked up a mouthful of salad greens. "How much do I owe you for lunch?" she asked.

"My treat." Suzanne waved a hand, munching on her own leaves. "It's nice for healthy food, but I don't think anything can beat one of those Seattle burgers."

"They were the best," Maddie reminisced.

"We'll have to go there again – soon." Suzanne's face lit up at the thought.

"Definitely!"

After she finished her salad, Maddie nibbled on her cookie. It was definitely tasty, despite being healthy. Ever since she and Suzanne had catered for the organic vegan self-help retreat, she'd been more adventurous with healthy, unusual foods.

"Hmm." Suzanne stared at her half-eaten cookie. "Maybe I could make a health ball version of this."

"Isn't that copying?" Maddie frowned.

"Huh. Maybe." Suzanne wrinkled her nose. "I might have to do some experimenting and see what I can come up with that's totally original and *not* copying."

"Good idea," Maddie replied with a little smile.

"Although," Suzanne continued, "I might have to put my experimenting to one side for now. I'll be over at your place tonight for the full moon, and we also have to find out who killed Veronica."

"No, we don't," Maddie replied. "You heard what Detective Edgewater said. We should stay out of it. And I think he might have a point."

"You do?" Suzanne stared at her, disappointment written on her face.

"Yes." Maddie nodded. "I don't think I heard one nice thing said about Veronica. We've personally heard from three women who had a grudge against her. How many more people did Veronica betray in some way? I really don't think we should get involved."

"Trixie?" Suzanne turned to the cat, but the Persian was busy nosing about in

her bowl for the last of the kibble.
Suzanne pouted.

"I can understand if you want to find out who did it because you were the one who found her," Maddie said gently.

"Yes." Suzanne nodded.

"But do you really want to get mixed up in murder again?"

"But we're good at it," Suzanne protested. "We've solved what – five murders in the past year so far?"

"Helped solve," Maddie corrected. "Detective Edgewater seems to know what he's doing."

"Sometimes," Suzanne countered.

"Well, he did say if we heard anything pertaining to Veronica to pass it on to him. So we could do that."

"Hmm." Suzanne made it sound very similar to Trixie's *"Broomf!"*

"Besides," Maddie tried to cajole her, "don't you have Ramon to dream about?"

CHAPTER 9

That evening, Suzanne arrived at Maddie's house.

"I can't wait to see what new spell you'll be able to do tonight," Suzanne enthused as she peered out of the living room window. The sky was black and the moon was heavy and golden. She pulled the curtains and turned around to face Maddie and Trixie, her eyes sparkling.

"Mrrow," Trixie seemed to agree, sitting on the periwinkle sofa next to *Wytchcraft for the Chosen*.

"I guess we'd better get started." Maddie sat on the other side of the book, while Suzanne sat next to Trixie.

Maddie opened the ancient tome, the pages crumbling and fly-spotted.

"You already know how to do the Tell the Truth spell," Suzanne mused. She suddenly drew in a breath. "I know! You could cast it on Ramon and ask him if he's really interested in me!"

"Suzanne." Maddie shook her head. "You know I don't agree with using magic for personal gain."

"It wouldn't be *your* personal gain," Suzanne argued. Her face fell as she reluctantly conceded Maddie's point, and she sighed.

"Mrrow." Trixie patted a page.

"You know how to do this one," Suzanne said. "Escape Your Enemy."

"Yes," Maddie replied, hoping she would never have to use it again.

They paged past glamour spells, fountain of youth spells, how to ensure a good harvest, and many others. But none of them appealed to Maddie. She knew from experience that she would experience a slight tug or inclination to a certain spell in the book – but only on the night of a full moon.

They were nearly at the end of the book. What if none of the spells called out to her tonight? Did that mean that her progress as a witch was suspended – or even halted?

"Mrrow." Trixie tapped the book with her paw, which meant, *"Turn the page."*

"Okay." Lately Maddie had been growing in confidence with her magical abilities, but tonight her doubts had resurfaced.

Why couldn't there be a page in the book that stated exactly what she could expect from her abilities in the coming years? The only reference she had was that when a witch turned seven-and-twenty, she came into her full powers. Maddie had turned twenty-seven months ago and so far was only able to master one new spell per month.

Maddie scanned the next page and paused. There was something different about this spell.

"An Incantation to Find Someone and Discover What They're Doing Right Now," she read out slowly.

"Mrrow," Trixie sounded approving.

"Ooh, is this the one?" Suzanne's face lit up.

"Maybe," Maddie replied cautiously.

"That sounds exciting!" Suzanne peered at the page.

Maddie studied the handwritten words on the page. Somehow, she knew that this was the spell she was meant to find tonight.

"You should try it now." Suzanne's eyes sparkled.

"Do you think so?"

"Mrrow!" Trixie agreed.

Maddie pulled out a small notebook and pen she had in her shorts' pocket. She knew from experience that it would be best if she wrote down the words so she wouldn't have to memorize the incantation and possibly make an error – with unintended results – when using it for the first time. But writing down the spell meant she'd have to make sure she had the scrap of paper on her everywhere, in case she needed to use it. And in the past, sometimes she'd had to use a spell when she'd least expected to, when she and Suzanne were investigating a murder.

"Mrrow." Trixie bunted her arm in approval as Maddie wrote down the words.

"Who are you going to spy on?" Suzanne asked eagerly.

"Hmm." Maddie nibbled her lip. Was it fair to spy on someone when it wasn't connected to solving a murder? Should they even get involved in attempting to solve Veronica's death? She glanced at Suzanne who looked like she wanted to bounce with excitement at the idea of Maddie attempting a new spell.

"What if I try it on you?" Maddie asked.

"Ooh!" Suzanne jumped up. "But you already know I'm standing right here."

"What if you go into my bedroom?" Maddie suggested. "And I'll cast the spell here."

"Okay." Suzanne hurried down the hall toward Maddie's room. "And I'm going to be doing something!" she called out.

Maddie gave her friend another minute, then read out the words on the paper. Trixie rubbed her cheek against Maddie's arm.

"Show me the person I am thinking of
Show me their actions
Show me true"

Maddie repeated the words three times while thinking of Suzanne. She tried not to let herself think that Suzanne was in her bedroom; instead, she focused her mind on the moment when Suzanne had jumped up from the sofa, excited about the spell.

A picture arose in her mind. Suzanne was in Maddie's bedroom, touching her toes.

Maddie giggled.

"It worked!" she called out.

"Mrrow!" Trixie agreed, hopping off the sofa and scampering toward Maddie's room. She followed her familiar.

"Well?" Suzanne flung open Maddie's bedroom door.

"You were touching your toes."

"Yes!" Suzanne hugged Maddie, and bent down to stroke Trixie. "It worked!"

***

Buzz buzz.

Maddie groaned and rolled over. She wished she could sleep in, especially after testing the incantation last night – she'd felt more tired than usual after Suzanne had gone home. But today was Friday.

She smiled, sleepily opening her eyes. That meant in two days' time she and

Trixie would be having a picnic with Luke.

"Mrrow." Trixie hopped onto her chest and gently patted Maddie's cheek, her claws sheathed. *Wake up.*

"Okay," Maddie grumbled good-humoredly.

After a quick breakfast and shower, Maddie and Trixie hopped in the truck and drove to the town square. Even though she had permission to park at the square during the day, she had to bring the truck home at night.

"Hi!" Suzanne waved and bounced on the spot as Maddie parked Brewed from the Bean.

"You're in a good mood," Maddie observed as she and Trixie jumped out of the front of the vehicle.

"I'm seeing Ramon tomorrow." Suzanne grinned. "I couldn't sleep last night after I got home, so I went through my closet and I've already picked out what to wear on my date!"

"That's great!"

"I even took a photo to show you – and Trixie." Suzanne held out her phone to both of them. A cute light blue dress with a swing skirt lay on her bedspread.

"I think it's perfect," Maddie said, pleased that her friend seemed calm – albeit enthusiastic – about her upcoming date.

"Me too," Suzanne said with satisfaction. "What about you, Trix?"

"Mrrow!" Trixie stared at the photo on the phone, putting out a paw to touch it.

"Oh, good." Suzanne put the phone back in her pocket. "Now all we have to do is catch the killer and have fabulous love lives!"

Maddie shook her head, choosing not to reply to Suzanne's remark. She jumped into the back of the truck and started setting up the coffee machine. In a few minutes, hopefully the early morning joggers would start arriving demanding bottled water, or for some of them, a quick espresso before they set off around the block again.

After selling five bottles of water in ten minutes, Maddie turned to Suzanne only to be interrupted by a nasal voice.

"I want to talk to you, Maddie Goodwell!" Claudine.

"What does she want?" Suzanne muttered, peering out through the serving hatch.

Claudine stood at the counter, dressed in black, her hands on her hips and a big scowl on her face.

"What did you do to my cousin?"

CHAPTER 10

"I'm sorry about Veronica," Maddie said awkwardly.

Trixie sat on her stool and stared at Claudine with narrowed eyes, but didn't say anything.

"Yes." Suzanne nodded.

"I just spent all yesterday afternoon being interrogated." Claudine scowled. "I don't know what you told that detective, but he didn't believe a word I said."

"What *did* you say?" Suzanne asked curiously.

"None of your coffee beans," Claudine snapped. "But I *did not* have anything to do with Veronica's death. How could I? She was my cousin!"

"Family members have killed before," Suzanne observed.

"Suzanne!" Maddie hissed out of the side of her mouth.

"Sorry." Suzanne looked abashed.

"We didn't say anything to Detective Edgewater," Maddie told Claudine as gently as she could. "He asked if we knew if Veronica had had an argument with anyone and we told him how you told Veronica to take down her iced coffee stand."

Maddie could tell by the look on Suzanne's face that she wanted to chime in with "*illegal* iced coffee stand" but to her friend's credit, she didn't say anything.

"What else?" Claudine demanded.

"That's it," Maddie told her.

"Then why did he question me over and over?" Claudine growled.

"Search me." Suzanne shrugged. "But we don't know anything else."

"I didn't kill her," Claudine told them. "But I don't know about you two. Do you have an alibi for the time of Veronica's death?"

Maddie and Suzanne looked at each other, their eyes wide. Detective Edgewater hadn't asked them that question.

"None of your business," Suzanne finally told her, but the snap was missing from her voice. "Do you?"

"Ha! As if I'd tell you." Claudine glowered. "But I know you two didn't like Veronica and I made sure I told the detective that."

"What?" Now it was Suzanne's turn to scowl at their nemesis. "You must know we didn't kill her."

"I don't know anything of the sort," Claudine huffed. "Just stay away from me – and my café. I don't even want to see you walk past the front *or* the back entrance." She turned to leave, a tiny tear glistening from her eye.

"Now I feel terrible," Maddie said when they were alone.

"I know what you mean." Suzanne sank on a stool. "I wish I hadn't been so … so … with her."

"She must have liked Veronica," Maddie continued. "Did you see Claudine's face just now?"

"Yeah." Suzanne nodded, her ponytail not bouncing. "I feel like a heel."

They turned to look at Trixie, but she just sat on her stool looking thoughtful.

"We don't even know when Veronica was killed," Suzanne said. "Detective Edgewater didn't tell us."

"We couldn't possibly be considered suspects, could we?" Now it was

Maddie's turn to flop on a stool. It wouldn't be the first time if they were.

A wave of customers came toward the truck.

"Let's try not to think about it right now." Suzanne stood, her fingers poised over the register.

"Good idea," Maddie agreed. Veronica hadn't seemed like a nice person, but no one deserved to be murdered.

***

"Vanilla cappuccino, detective?" Suzanne asked later that morning. They were enjoying a welcome respite from customers. Today's business had already made up for the downturn in sales that week. Iced mochas were a hit!

"Not today, thank you, Suzanne," Detective Edgewater said, plucking his notebook from his coat pocket.

"Mrrow," Trixie said quietly.

She'd hardly said anything all morning – ever since Claudine had visited them. Was she thinking about the murder? Or had Claudine distressed her

112

in some way? Maddie didn't think the Persian had forgotten the way Claudine had treated her when she'd appeared in the café over a year ago.

"Hello, Trixie." The detective's solemn face lightened a little as he looked at the furry white cat.

Trixie lifted a paw in his direction, then settled on her stool.

"Have you two forgotten to tell me something?" he asked enquiringly.

Maddie and Suzanne looked at each other in puzzlement.

"No sir," Maddie replied.

"Nope." Suzanne's ponytail swished.

"I've been told that you hated the victim and wanted her dead," he continued.

"Who told you that?" Suzanne's eyebrows climbed to her hairline.

"It's not true," Maddie said quietly.

"Where were you around seven o'clock yesterday morning?" he asked.

"At home," Maddie answered. "And then Trixie and I left around 7.20 and drove the truck here."

"And I left my house about that same time and arrived just after Maddie," Suzanne added.

"We open at 7.30 Monday to Saturday," Maddie said.

"Sometimes a few minutes earlier," Suzanne chimed in.

"Okay." He wrote something down. "I hope you know I didn't like asking you that, but it's my job." He frowned. "And you're sure you don't have anything to add to what you told me yesterday about the victim?"

"Like what?" Suzanne crinkled her brow.

"Did you have a reason to hate Veronica? I know she was encroaching on your territory."

"Claudine was also trying to," Maddie told him.

"But we put a stop to it," Suzanne said. Her mouth dropped open as she realized what she'd said and she paled. "Not like that," she said hastily.

"Suzanne wouldn't harm a fly," Maddie said loyally. "After Claudine set up her iced coffee stand, the mayor stopped by and said he'd received a complaint – not by us–"

"Although we were about to complain to *him*," Suzanne interrupted.

"The mayor told Claudine she couldn't set up outside her café," Maddie continued. "And then Veronica tried to set up next to us and that's when Claudine came over to tell her to pull down her stand."

"And that's all the interaction we've had with Veronica," Suzanne said.

"That tallies with what you told me yesterday." The detective tucked his notebook back in his pocket.

"So Veronica was killed at seven a.m.?" Maddie asked.

"Around that time, it looks like," he agreed.

"Claudine's café isn't open that early," Suzanne said thoughtfully.

"Mmm." He nodded. "So I've been told."

After advising them once more to stay focused on their own business and not Veronica's murder, he departed.

"Phew! I think he believes our alibis," Suzanne said.

"I hope so." Maddie nibbled her lip.

"Mrrow," Trixie said quietly.

"He has to – because they're true," Suzanne declared. "I think I need an iced mocha. Want me to make you one too?"

"I'll make them," Maddie replied.

Suzanne knew how to work the coffee machine, and she made a decent coffee, but her friend was the first to admit that Maddie had far better barista skills.

"I'll squirt the cream on them." Suzanne smiled, then sobered. "I feel guilty even smiling. I can't believe Claudine threw us under the espresso machine like that."

"She probably thinks we did that to her," Maddie said thoughtfully as she turned her attention to the machine. The familiar hissing and grinding soothed her nerves.

"We didn't tell Detective Edgewater anything that wasn't public knowledge – if members of the public were out in the town square and overheard what happened with Veronica and the coffee stand."

"I know," Maddie agreed. "But Claudine probably doesn't see it that way."

"Mrrow," Trixie agreed.

"Are you okay, Trix?" Suzanne gently stroked the Persian. "You've been very quiet this morning."

"Mrrow." Trixie seemed to nod. Then she curled up in a ball, tucked her nose to her tail and closed her eyes.

"Maybe she's thinking about things," Maddie suggested as she handed over two icy concoctions to Suzanne.

Suzanne picked up the stainless-steel canister and squirted a mound of cream on each drink.

"Suzanne!" Maddie's mouth parted as she stared at the huge pile of cream on top of the beverages. "Is there any cream left for the customers?"

"Yep." Suzanne opened the refrigerator door. Three cartons of cream stared at them. "Plenty. And it's not so hot today, so we might sell more hot drinks than cold. Ooh! Maybe we could offer whipped cream on top of the hot coffees."

"In this weather?" Maddie wrinkled her brow. "It might appeal in winter, but in summer …?"

"We can make it a special." Suzanne stuck two straws in the iced mochas and handed one to Maddie. "Drink up before we get any customers and I'll write it up on the specials board, under our new iced mochas."

The rest of the morning went smoothly. Word must have gotten around about the two new additions to the menu, because by mid-afternoon they were out of whipped cream.

"I'd better run to the store and grab some more cream." Suzanne grinned. "I think we're making more money with these two new drinks than with health balls!"

"But people love your healthy treats," Maddie said. "Someone usually asks at least once per day about them."

"I know." Suzanne sobered. "And I'll get back to making them when the weather is cooler. In the meantime, I'm going to think up some new variations."

"Good idea." Maddie smiled at her bestie.

118

Since they didn't have any customers at the moment, Suzanne dashed off to the grocery store. A lot of their regulars had spoken about the murder, still curious as to who could have done such a terrible thing. Maddie had wanted to ask a couple of them some questions, but had held back, mindful of Detective Edgewater's warning. Surely the sheriff's department could handle the investigation?

CHAPTER 11

On Sunday, Luke picked up Maddie and Trixie. They drove to a small park on the edge of town. Tall green pine trees guarded the perimeter, while picnic benches and green grass – still lush even in the warm weather – invited one to sit and relax and enjoy an alfresco meal.

Maddie had brought a large blanket and Luke helped her smooth it over the grass. They had a spot all to themselves. In the distance children played on the swings, and an occasional bird chirped.

Maddie felt the weight of the events of last week lift off her shoulders. Trixie wore her turquoise harness and settled down on the red-checked blanket, rolling on her back and exposing her white tummy to the sun.

"She's cute." Luke smiled at the Persian.

"And I think she knows it." Maddie stifled a giggle.

"You're cute too." Luke sat down next to her and traced his finger along her cheekbone.

"So are you," Maddie whispered, before his mouth met hers.

After a couple of minutes, a loud "Mrrow!" interrupted them.

"I think Trixie's saying she's hungry," Maddie said ruefully as they broke apart, the imprint of Luke's lips on hers sending a tingle down her spine.

"Here you go, Trixie." She reached into the cooler and opened a container containing chicken in gravy.

Trixie bunted Maddie's arm in thanks, then delicately licked off the gravy as if it were the finest meal she'd ever eaten.

"I guess we'd better eat too," Luke said wryly, helping Maddie take the rest of the food out of the cooler.

They lunched on cold fried chicken, coleslaw, and fresh bread rolls. Maddie had packed strawberries for dessert, as well as water and freshly squeezed lemonade. After all the coffee she'd drunk last week, she thought she'd have a caffeine-free day. She hadn't counted on Luke's kisses having a similar effect.

After Trixie finished her lunch, she lay down on the blanket again, a contented look on her face.

"We should do this more often," Luke commented once they'd eaten the last of the strawberries.

"Definitely," Maddie agreed.

"Mrrow," Trixie said softly, before closing her eyes and dozing.

Maddie and Luke spoke quietly about their plans for the next few weeks, then somehow the talk turned to Veronica's murder.

"I'm glad you and Suzanne aren't considered suspects," he said.

"Me too."

"Veronica returning to Estherville obviously stirred up some deep-seated resentment," he continued.

Maddie stared at him. "You think so?"

He nodded. "I had a customer grumbling to me about it a couple of days ago."

"What did he say?"

"Not much." He shrugged. "Just that he was surprised she was back after the way she'd burned people in high school."

"Has Detective Edgewater spoken to him?" Maddie asked.

"I don't know." He scrutinized her. "You're not going to get involved in this, are you?"

"I don't want to, but …" How could she explain to him what she could barely put into words to herself? There was a certain satisfaction in bringing a killer to justice, and in the past, she and Suzanne – and Trixie – had helped to do just that. But Detective Edgewater's warning rang in her mind. After a few close calls in the past, did she really want to involve herself in someone else's business – murderous business – again?

"Promise me you'll be careful," Luke told her. "I don't want anything happening to you or my sister. Or Trixie." He glanced fondly at the stretched-out feline, snoozing contentedly in the sun.

As if she heard her name, Trixie blinked and slowly opened her eyes. She rolled over, this time angling her body into a spot of shade provided by the large branches of a pine tree nearby, before closing her eyes and dozing once more.

Maddie envied her the ability to do that. Her familiar looked like she didn't have a care in the world.

"I promise," she said softly, glad that somehow Luke seemed to understand her dilemma.

"What about this Ramon guy?" he asked. "Do you trust him?"

"Yes." She nodded. "We've known him for a while now. And Trixie likes him."

Luke smiled as he looked over at the cat. "Then maybe my sister is safe with him."

"I think Suzanne can look after herself," Maddie tried to reassure him.

Suzanne had called her late yesterday afternoon, bubbling over about her lunch date with Ramon. Maddie had found it difficult to get a word in, until her friend finally ran out of breath – and voice.

"I hope so." Luke grew serious. "I know she's a grown woman, but she's my sister and always will be."

"Maybe if you meet him ...?" Maddie suggested slowly, an idea forming in her mind. "What if you're at Brewed from the Bean at the same time as Ramon? He usually stops by a few times per week to grab a coffee."

"You're a genius." Luke pressed a swift kiss on her lips.

"I'll text you next time he's at the truck," Maddie replied, a soft smile on her face.

A couple of hours later, Luke drove Maddie and Trixie home. The Persian scampered inside the house, curling up on the sofa, (*Wytchcraft for the Chosen* out of sight) while Maddie made Luke a latte. Instead of caffeine, she enjoyed some lemonade left over from lunch.

After confirming plans for dinner on Tuesday, Luke left.

Maddie sighed after him as she watched him get into his tan SUV. She felt like echoing Suzanne when she spoke about Ramon at times.

I'm so going to marry that man one day.

Before or after she told him she was a witch?

CHAPTER 12

To keep her mind off Luke, all Sunday evening Maddie thought about the murder. She didn't know if that was better or worse.

Disquiet began to gnaw at her when she realized she and Suzanne hadn't done anything to investigate Veronica's death.

Would they really put themselves in danger if they asked a few discreet questions? Surely just doing that wouldn't hinder Detective Edgewater's investigation – would it?

"Mrrow," Trixie said softly as Maddie stroked her. They sat on the sofa in the living room.

"Do you think it's a good idea to look into Veronica's death?" Maddie asked her.

"Mrrow." Trixie sounded serious.

Was that a yes or a no? Sometimes she was sure she could decipher Trixie's meows but right now, her familiar's answer had her puzzled.

Perhaps it was up to Maddie to decide what it meant. And right now, it meant *Yes*.

As Maddie brushed her teeth and got into her summer pjs, there was only one thing on her mind. Tomorrow she'd tell Suzanne that they needed to investigate Veronica's murder.

***

"And then I ordered chicken marsala, and Ramon said I had to try a little of his beef burgundy." Suzanne's face sparkled as Maddie turned on the espresso machine Monday morning.

"I know." Maddie grinned. "You told me on the phone Saturday."

"But now I'm telling you in person!" Suzanne bounced on the balls of her feet. "Oh, Mads, I had such a wonderful time! Ramon is so awesome – even more awesome than I first thought!"

"Did he kiss you?" Maddie asked curiously. That was the one detail Suzanne hadn't mentioned. Instantly, she regretted asking. "Sorry. Forget I asked."

Some things were private. That was how she'd felt when Luke had first kissed her.

"You know I'd tell you if he did," Suzanne told her. Her expression dimmed a little. "No, he hasn't yet. But that's okay. It means when he does, it's going to be – oh, I can't even think of the words to describe what it will be like!"

Wow. Maddie couldn't remember the last time she'd heard Suzanne rave about a guy like this. She just hoped everything worked out between her friend and Ramon. She didn't want her friend to be crushed if it didn't.

Trixie had been listening intently to Suzanne, her ears pricked and her expression alert.

"Mrrow!" She now chimed in, as if agreeing with Suzanne's last sentence.

"I'm so glad you agree, Trix." Suzanne giggled as she shared a look of understanding with the cat.

Did Trixie have some magical intuition going on about Suzanne's and Ramon fledgling romantic relationship? Maddie hoped so.

Just then, an influx of sweaty joggers claimed their attention. After their customers departed, Maddie turned to her friend.

"I've been thinking," she said. "I don't see how it could hurt if we asked a few careful questions – about Veronica."

"Me too!" Suzanne high-fived her. "I think it's wrong if we don't do something to help. What does Trixie say?"

Maddie looked at her familiar. Trixie looked back at her, an inscrutable expression on her face.

"I think Trixie will agree with whatever we decide," she said, feeling her way.

"Mrrow." Trixie seemed to nod.

"Oh good." Suzanne grinned. "Now, let's get started. Who should we interview first?"

"It's more a few discreet questions instead of an interview," Maddie cautioned.

"Oh, pooh." Suzanne waved a hand in the air. "If we're going to solve this murder, I think we'll have to do more than just a couple of questions. Don't you agree, Trix?"

"Mrrow." Trixie seemed to agree.

"We still need to be careful." Maddie voiced her concern.

"We will be," Suzanne promised. "But if we don't ask enough questions, we won't get enough answers. And one of those answers could lead us to the killer!"

***

Just before lunch, Maddie and Suzanne sat down during a lull and discussed who to question first.

Suzanne pulled out her phone. "Let me make some notes." She pressed some buttons on her cell. "Okay. Go."

"Who had a grudge against Veronica?" Maddie mused.

"Grace. Veronica stole her boyfriend thirty-two years ago." Suzanne made a note. "And Pamela. Veronica stole her spot on the cheerleading squad in high school."

"There seems to be a theme," Maddie said wryly.

"And Amy!" Suzanne made another note on her phone. "Veronica got her expelled from school so—"

"She could steal Amy's college scholarship."

"Veronica was *not* a nice person," Suzanne stated. "Not then, anyway."

"And she didn't seem very nice when we met her," Maddie replied, disliking having to say such a thing. Even if it were true.

"Who else?" Suzanne drummed her fingertips on her phone screen.

"Oh." Maddie straightened. "Luke told me yesterday that one of his customers spoke about Veronica last week."

"What did he say?"

"Only that he was surprised Veronica had returned to Estherville after what she got up to in high school."

"Anything else?"

"No." Maddie sighed.

"I'll put that in as *Unknown male who seemed to know her in high school, ask Luke for more info*." Suzanne punched the buttons on her phone.

"So who should we start with?" Maddie asked. "There are four people to talk to."

131

"Amy, who works at the supermarket, is the closest," Suzanne replied. "I know!" She snapped her fingers. "When we run out of cream today, I'll go to the grocery store and see if I can grab her for a few minutes and ask her some questions."

"Maybe we should both go," Maddie suggested, aware that sometimes Suzanne's enthusiastic questioning could get a little out of hand.

"Okay." Suzanne's ponytail bobbed. "It won't hurt to close the truck for a few minutes when it's quiet."

"Mrrow," Trixie agreed.

"I hope we run out of cream." Maddie stared through the serving hatch. No customers.

"Maybe we should eat our lunch while we can." Suzanne retrieved her sandwich from the fridge.

"Good idea," Maddie replied as her stomach gurgled.

After giving Trixie crunchy chicken flavored kibble, Maddie unwrapped her turkey and lettuce sandwich. She'd just taken a bite when she spied Detective Edgewater walking toward the truck.

"Look!" She put down her lunch. "We can tell the detective about Luke's customer who was complaining—"

"—about Veronica," Suzanne finished for her.

"Hi, detective," Suzanne greeted him. "What can we get you?"

"Got any health balls?" He looked hopefully at the counter, but it was empty apart from the little specials blackboard and an array of condiments, such as straws.

"Not right now," Suzanne replied. "But you haven't tried our new specials!" She gestured to the blackboard as if she were a game show presenter. "Everyone's raving about the iced mocha and the whipped cream topping for the usual coffees."

"Hmm." He narrowed his eyes, as if he couldn't make up his mind. "Since it's summer, I'll try the iced mocha."

"Coming right up," Maddie promised, preparing an espresso shot.

"I'm glad you're here," Suzanne told him. "We've got some information for you."

"You haven't been poking around, have you?" he asked.

"No." Suzanne shook her head. "My brother told Maddie who told me. And now we're telling you."

"Go on."

Suzanne told him about Luke's customer who'd grumbled about Veronica coming back to town.

"Got a name?" Detective Edgewater asked.

"No. Sorry," Maddie said as she handed the plastic cup over to Suzanne to decorate with the cream.

Suzanne seemed to delight in squirting a very unhealthy amount of cream on top of the icy mocha.

"Here you go, detective." She slid the drink toward him. "You're going to love it."

"If I don't have a heart attack first." He eyed the frosty concoction skeptically, then stuck in a straw and sipped. His face brightened. "That *is* good. But next time, lighter on the cream, please. I'm not as young as I used to be." He patted his chest.

After thanking them for the tidbit of information, the detective left, sipping on his beverage.

"Another satisfied customer." Suzanne flopped on her stool and picked up her sandwich.

"He was right about the cream," Maddie observed. "You were a little heavy handed."

"And that's how we're going to run out of cream before closing this afternoon," Suzanne said smugly. "So when we talk to Amy we won't be lying."

A reluctant smile appeared on Maddie's lips and she shook her head. "I should have known."

"Yep." Suzanne took a bite of her chicken sandwich.

They just had time to eat their lunch before workers in need of lunchtime caffeine descended on the truck. Both their specials were hits once more, and Maddie noticed out of the corner of her eye as she worked the machine that Suzanne had stopped being so liberal with the whipped cream. That must mean they were in danger of running out.

Once their customers had departed to their workplaces, Maddie saw Ramon head across the town square toward them. She had to tell Luke!

Pulling her phone out of her pocket, she texted him, hoping Suzanne wouldn't see what she was doing. Maddie was in luck. Suzanne looked through the serving hatch, standing stock still.

"Hi Ramon," she greeted the gorgeous Spaniard in a dreamy voice.

"Hello, Suzanne."

There was silence for a moment. Maddie looked up from her phone. The two of them stared at each other across the counter.

"Mrrow!"

"Hello, Trixie." Ramon blinked as he seemed to become aware of his surroundings. "And Maddie."

"Hi." Maddie smiled at him. When Suzanne didn't say anything, just continued to gaze at Ramon, Maddie said, "Would you like an espresso?"

"Yes, please," he replied.

Maddie pulled the shot, aware of Suzanne and Ramon talking softly. She smiled to herself. Her bestie really had it bad. And it looked like she wasn't the only one affected, judging by Ramon's behavior.

Her eyes widened as she saw Luke hurry toward the truck. For a second, she wondered if she'd done the right thing by engineering this meeting. She just hoped Suzanne would forgive her if it hadn't been the best idea.

"Hi, Sis," Luke said loudly when he arrived at the counter, standing next to Ramon. They were practically the same height, although Luke was dressed down in comparison, wearing jeans and a navy t-shirt, while Ramon wore tailored chinos and a blue shirt.

"Oh. Hi." Suzanne blinked, as if coming out of a trance. "Want your usual?"

"Hello." Ramon turned to Luke. "I have been looking forward to meeting you. I am Ramon."

"Luke." He nodded. "You work across the square, don't you?"

"That is correct. I am a masseur."

Luke made a non-committal sound.

"Ramon gives the best massages," Suzanne enthused, apparently unaware

137

that her brother didn't seem impressed by Ramon's profession. "Doesn't he, Mads?"

"So you tell me," Maddie replied, aware of the expression on Luke's face. He looked as if he'd just been beaned by a bag of coffee. "I haven't had one."

"You must one day," Ramon told her. "I know you work hard, Maddie. A nice, soothing massage with relaxing essential oils will make you feel wonderful."

Maddie nodded, her cheeks heating. She had been too shy to try a massage with the Spaniard, even though Suzanne had raved about it afterward. And since she and Luke had started dating, Maddie hadn't felt the need to avail herself of Ramon's services, even though Suzanne had assured her he was strictly professional and highly qualified.

Maddie finished making the Spaniard's coffee, then started on an icy mocha, making sure she put plenty of chocolate powder in it. Perhaps some cocoa goodness would help cheer up her boyfriend.

"Just give me my usual," Luke said tightly.

"Too late," Maddie told him. She nudged Suzanne. "This is my treat," she whispered.

Suzanne looked a little surprised but nodded. Luke always made a point of paying for his coffee, saying he didn't want to take advantage of his sister or Maddie. Ramon always paid for his coffee as well, and Suzanne paid for her massages. The system seemed to work well for all of them.

"Mrrow?" Trixie inquired, staring at Luke.

"I'm okay, Trixie," he reassured the cat, his expression lightening a tad.

Suzanne added a big mound of cream to the icy concoction and handed it to her brother, waving away his cash. "Talk to Maddie about it – later," she added as a few customers came toward their truck.

Luke smiled a thank you to Maddie, but his expression looked wary as he gave Ramon a parting glance.

Oh no. Had Maddie done the right thing by engineering a meeting between the two men?

CHAPTER 13

They ran out of cream at three
o'clock. Luckily, there were no
customers, so Maddie clipped on Trixie's
harness and they closed the truck,
Suzanne sticking a *"Back in ten minutes"*
sign in the window.

"I don't think five minutes will be
long enough," she said in reply to
Maddie's questioning glance.

They walked across the square to the
small supermarket. It carried nearly
everything they needed for their own
groceries, and just about everything
Suzanne needed for her health balls.

"There she is!" Suzanne muttered to
Maddie as they entered the store. Amy
was restocking the milk. "Perfect. The
cream is right next to her."

"What are we going to ask her?"
Maddie whispered. After Ramon and
Luke had departed, they'd been busy with
customers and hadn't had time to develop
a plan.

"I'll think of something," Suzanne
said airily.

Maddie gulped. That's what she was afraid of.

"Hi, Amy." Suzanne grinned at the older woman.

"Hi, girls. Hi, Trixie." The older woman bent down to say hello to the Persian. "How are you?"

"Mrrow," Trixie replied politely.

"I'd love to have a cat one day," Amy said wistfully as she straightened.

"Is there any reason you can't have one now?" Maddie asked.

"My landlord won't allow it." Amy grimaced.

"Oh." Maddie was glad her landlord *did* allow cats.

"Pooh." Suzanne frowned in sympathy. "You should stop by for one of our specials to cheer yourself up. I'll put extra cream on for you."

"I've heard about your iced mochas and whipped cream toppings. Maybe I will." Amy did look slightly happier at the thought. "Do you girls need any help here?"

"Just stocking up on more cream." Suzanne picked up a basket. "So many of our customers can't believe Veronica was murdered." She tsked.

Maddie didn't think it was much of a segue but Amy didn't seem to notice.

"The whole town is talking about it," Amy replied. "Veronica was a nasty piece of work but I didn't expect her to be murdered." She didn't sound very sorrowful about it, though.

Suzanne cast a sideways glance at Maddie, as if she didn't want Maddie to miss her cue. Feeling slightly shady, Maddie said, "Suzanne found the – Veronica's body."

"No!" Amy stared at Suzanne, her mouth parted. "I hadn't heard. How terrible!"

"It was." Suzanne shuddered, and Maddie didn't think she was acting.

"Tell me *everything*." Amy leaned forward, her eyes bright with curiosity.

"We were walking at the rear of—" Suzanne was interrupted by a twenty-something guy with acne on his cheeks. *John – Acting Manager* was emblazoned on the badge pinned to his shirt.

"You're not paid to stand around gossiping with customers, Amy," he told her shortly. "After you restock the milk I need you to fix the dogfood display – some kid knocked all the cans down." He looked as if he wanted to exile children to the nastiest place on earth – forever. "And then you can go out back and start unloading the pallets of cookies."

"It's my fault." Suzanne frowned at the guy. "I was asking Amy which brand of cream she recommended."

The acting manager scanned the cartons of cream in Suzanne's basket. "Then she should have told you to buy the other brand. It's more expensive." He gave Amy a dark look and stalked off.

"Wow." Suzanne shook her head in disgust. "What a jerk!"

"He's like that all the time," Amy said bitterly. "If I didn't need this job, I'd tell him to get lost." She hesitated. "If Veronica hadn't stolen that scholarship from me, I wouldn't have to put up with this – heck, I probably wouldn't be working here. I'd have a big city job somewhere making a lot more money."

"I'm sorry," Maddie said sympathetically.

"Mrrow." Trixie sounded sorry, too.

"It is what it is." Amy sighed. "But if you ask me, someone did the world a favor by killing Veronica."

CHAPTER 14

On Tuesday night, Maddie got ready for her date with Luke.

She and Suzanne had discussed who they should talk to next, but that was as far as they'd gotten – apart from agreeing they were glad they owned Brewed from the Bean, so they didn't have to put up with anyone bossing them around. Maddie hadn't been able to stop her slight smile during their conversation – somctimes Suzanne bossed *her* around, although she didn't seem to realize – most of the time.

As she brushed her hair, Trixie watching intently, Maddie's stomach tightened. Luke hadn't seemed very impressed with meeting Ramon yesterday. Would he blame her for setting up the meeting?

She needn't have worried.

Over dinner at the steakhouse in a neighboring town, Luke looked at her appreciatively over the blue checkered tablecloth.

"Thanks for letting me know Ramon was at the truck today," he said.

"You're welcome," Maddie replied softly. The atmosphere was quiet, the lights low, and the soft country rock background music seemed the perfect choice.

"One thing is bothering me," he continued. He looked around the room but the tables near them were unoccupied, although there were diners across the room.

"What is it?"

"Are his massages legit?" He kept his voice low as he leaned toward her.

Maddie bit her lip. It wasn't funny. Not really.

"Yes," she replied when she was able to do so without giggling. "Suzanne says they are."

"Good." He relaxed slightly.

"He *is* a qualified masseur."

"Good," he repeated. He hesitated. "And you haven't …?"

"No." She realized what he was trying to say and didn't think it fair to tease him.

"I'd understand if you needed to have a massage," he said.

"I don't need one at the moment," Maddie replied. An impish thought struck her. "But sometimes my shoulders get a little tight at the end of the day." True. "Maybe if you're—"

"Happy to be of service." His emerald gaze held hers for several beats and her cheeks heated.

They were interrupted by the server who delivered their entrees of rib eye steak for Luke and a petit filet for Maddie. Both dishes came with a baked potato and a garden salad full of colorful salad leaves with a honeyed pomegranate dressing.

While they ate, Maddie updated him on their investigation to date, not that there was much to tell him. Still, Luke asked her – and his sister – to be careful.

"Detective Edgewater said he visited your shop," Maddie said as they started on their dessert of chocolate mousse.

"Yeah. There wasn't much I could tell him, though. Apart from the name of my customer." Luke grimaced. "I just hope Eddie understands."

"If he's innocent, then I'm sure he will," Maddie tried to reassure him. "You don't mind us telling Detective Edgewater about it?"

"I kind of expected that to happen," Luke said. He offered her a half smile. "I guess it comes with the territory when my girlfriend is investigating a murder."

After dinner, Luke drove Maddie home, accepting her offer of a latte, and sitting next to her on the sofa in the living room.

Trixie greeted him with an affectionate "Mrrow," and joined them on the couch.

Wytchcraft for the Chosen was hidden in the bookshelf, out of sight.

After they told Trixie about dinner, Maddie and Luke chatted for a while, before Luke kissed her goodnight. After a few lingering kisses, Luke departed, leaving Maddie with a smile on her face.

***

The next morning, Maddie woke to find Trixie sitting on her chest.

"Mrrow." She blinked her turquoise eyes at Maddie, then jumped off.

Maddie staggered to the kitchen, still not fully awake. After giving Trixie beef in gravy, she walked past the living room on the way to her bedroom. *Wytchcraft for the Chosen* lay on the sofa.

She stopped and stared.

After Luke had departed last night, she and Trixie had gone to bed. How on earth had the book found its way onto the sofa?

"Trixie?" she called.

The feline sauntered out of the kitchen and looked up at her enquiringly.

"Did you have anything to do with this?" She gestured to the ancient tome, visible from the doorway.

"Mrrow." Trixie looked coy.

"Well, unless the book is able to move itself—" was it able to? "— I think you did." Maddie shook her head. Trixie constantly surprised her.

The sight of the book got Maddie thinking. Would she ever have a chance to use the new incantation she'd discovered on the night of the full moon? The spell to find a person and discover what they were up to at that very moment? Would it help them in some way discover who Veronica's killer was?

Was the fact that *Wytchcraft for the Chosen* was out in plain sight a hint that she should page through the book to see if there was anything else that would help them investigate the murder? Or was it on the sofa because Trixie wanted to look at it while Maddie was at work?

She hadn't found Trixie actually paging through the tome before, but she knew her familiar liked guarding it on the sofa, and she always seemed interested in looking at the pages when Maddie studied the book.

Maddie wasn't surprised when Trixie curled up on the sofa after breakfast, one paw on the old volume.

"Want to stay home today?" she asked the Persian.

"Mrrow," Trixie seemed to agree.

Maddie drove to the town square, not sure what to think about first. She was glad Luke accepted her curiosity about the murder, and her desire to help discover the killer. But there was also the fact that she and Suzanne needed to discuss who to question next. And, wondering if she could ever tell Luke that she was a witch. He really seemed to "get" her. Would he be able to accept her magical abilities as well?

Deciding to think about that difficult question another day, Maddie pulled up at the square, jumped out, and waved to Suzanne, who'd arrived before her.

"No Trixie?" Suzanne looked disappointed.

"She wanted to stay home and guard *Wytchcraft for the Chosen*," Maddie explained. She dug into her pocket and pulled out her phone. After tapping a button, she showed Suzanne the live camera feed of the living room. The Persian was curled up on the sofa next to the old book, seemingly asleep.

"Ohhhh." Suzanne smiled softly.

They set up the truck and waited for their first customer, a wiry jogger who'd forgotten his bottle of water. It had been Suzanne's idea early on to sell bottles of water for the early morning exercisers, and it had proven to be a hit.

After he'd run back across the square, Suzanne drummed her fingertips on the counter.

"Who should we question today?" she asked.

"We still have Grace and Pamela on the list," Maddie replied.

"Grace lives in that big old house on the edge of town," Suzanne said. "You know, the gorgeous old Victorian with the big garden."

"Yes, the pretty cream and yellow house," Maddie said. "I've always wondered what it's like inside."

"We should go and find out." Suzanne grinned.

"We'll have to close up the truck," Maddie warned.

"We've done that before," Suzanne reminded her. "It's a shame Trixie isn't with us, though. Everyone seems to like her and she seems to put people at ease."

"Apart from Claudine," Maddie said darkly.

"Yeah." Suzanne grimaced. "But it might do us good to have a little change of scene."

"Okay," Maddie agreed. "But we can't just knock on Grace's door and ask her pointed questions about Veronica's death."

"Can't we?" Suzanne wrinkled her nose.

"No," Maddie told her. "We need some sort of pretext."

"Ooh, I know." Suzanne snapped her fingers. "We could ask her questions about her garden. It worked in one of our other cases. People *love* talking about their garden. We could say we're thinking of seriously getting into gardening and wanted to ask her advice on … something."

"Let's decide on the prettiest flower she has out the front and ask her questions about that," Maddie proposed.

"Yes! And then we'll just slip in some questions about Veronica's murder."

"Like you did yesterday with Amy at the grocery?"

Suzanne wrinkled her brow. "I realize that wasn't my finest questioning, but it worked, didn't it?"

"Until her boss came along."

"Ugh." Suzanne frowned. "We didn't learn much from Amy, anyway. Apart from knowing she definitely had a motive for murder. I don't think I could stand to work with that guy for an hour, let alone *weeks* until her old boss gets back from vacation."

"I know," Maddie agreed. "But why would Amy kill Veronica now? Would that change her life for the better in any way?"

"Maybe not," Suzanne said thoughtfully. "But I think it would have given her a great deal of personal satisfaction."

CHAPTER 15

After the lunchtime rush had ended, Maddie penned a new sign – *Back at 3.30pm.* Surely that would give them enough time to drive to Grace's, interview her, and return to the town square?

Since they didn't feel like walking such a distance, they headed to Maddie's house to grab her car.

"Maybe Trixie will want to join us." Suzanne's eyes lit up.

"Good idea." Maddie smiled.

It seemed Trixie had used her intuition and knew about their plans because the feline was just inside the front door when Maddie unlocked it. Dangling from her mouth was a turquoise harness.

"Goody." Suzanne grinned at the feline. "I'm glad you're coming with us, Trix."

"Mrrow." Trixie seemed to have a smile on her face as Maddie buckled the harness around her body.

"We're going to Grace's house to ask her questions about Veronica," Maddie informed her familiar. "And we're going to look at her garden first."

"Mrrow!" It sounded like the feline version of Suzanne's "Goody!"

A few minutes later they arrived at Grace's house. A garden surrounded the large Victorian.

"She must have a couple of acres at least," Suzanne said admiringly. "Look at all those flowers!"

Blooms of all shapes, sizes, and colors decorated the front garden.

"I don't know which one I like the most," Maddie admitted as they hopped out of the car. "Be careful with the flowers, Trix," she told the cat. "Some flowers can make you very sick, like lilies."

"Mrrow," Trixie replied, her eyes wide as she stared at all the different plants.

Maddie had a small front and back lawn and a few shrubs. After Trixie entered her life, she'd researched dangerous plants for cats and was pleased to discover that everything in her garden was deemed safe.

They opened the cream wrought iron gate and stepped inside the garden.

"Ooh, orange honeysuckle!" Suzanne inspected the trailing vines. "It's gorgeous! I'm going to ask Grace about it."

"That was quick," Maddie said wryly, her attention caught by some pink dahlias further along that side of the garden. A blue and white marbled pot stood next to them in the corner, a chip marring its appearance.

"I really do like it," Suzanne said earnestly.

"Mrrow," Trixie agreed.

"Okay." Maddie smiled.

They trooped along the path to the porch.

Suzanne pressed the doorbell, a loud chime echoing inside.

"I hope she's home," Suzanne murmured. "I didn't notice a car in the driveway."

"Maybe it's in the garage," Maddie suggested, as she spotted a coach house in keeping with the Victorian look of the house. She assumed Grace used it as a garage.

The front door, decorated with stained glass inserts featuring red roses, opened noiselessly. Grace greeted them with surprise, looking cool in a cream shift dress.

"Maddie and Suzanne! And Trixie." She bent and smiled at the feline. "What are you doing here?"

"We've admired your garden for ages," Suzanne said. "And since we're thinking about getting into gardening, I wanted to ask you about your gorgeous orange honeysuckle." Suzanne pointed to the flower that had snagged her attention.

"Oh, yes, that's an Orange Trumpet Honeysuckle, and it's native to the area," the older woman replied. "Why don't I give you a cutting?"

"That's very kind of you," Maddie replied.

"Mrrow," Trixie seemed to agree.

"Yes," Suzanne added.

"I'll just get some shears." Grace disappeared inside the house.

"That was easy," Suzanne whispered.

"Shh." Maddie widened her eyes and tilted her head toward the open front door. She didn't want Grace to hear them, even if they were murmuring.

A minute later, Grace reappeared, a large pair of garden shears in her hand, the tips looking wickedly sharp.

"Is there anything else that's caught your eye?" she asked pleasantly as she led the way down the porch steps and toward the honeysuckle.

"Not really," Suzanne told her. "I mean, everything looks so pretty, but I think the honeysucklc will really suit my little garden."

Grace nodded as she cut a few different lengths of the vine and dug in her pocket for a brown paper bag.

"Here you go." She handed the bag to Suzanne with a smile. "Put each cutting in a small pot with some soil and make sure you water them regularly. Hopefully they'll take."

"Thanks. Did you hear about Veronica?" Suzanne asked. "Someone killed her."

"Yes." Grace nodded. "I heard." Her expression didn't give anything away.

"I hate to say this …" Suzanne seemed to pause for effect, "…but I was the one who found her."

"No!" Grace looked shocked. "I'm sorry, my dear."

"Thanks." Suzanne smiled wanly. "I guess that's what happens when you're curious and you look inside a garbage can."

"I don't know what the world is coming to." Grace tutted. "But Veronica wasn't a nice person. I'm not surprised in one way that she ended up being murdered."

"Really?" Maddie asked.

Sadness swept over Grace's expression. "She ruined my life – along with my father."

"Oh." Suzanne's eyes widened and Maddie was pretty sure it wasn't an act. "What happened?"

"You don't have to tell us," Maddie said quickly. "We don't mean to be nosy." It was one thing to ask questions, but she didn't want to intrude on the older woman's private thoughts.

"My friends know what happened, so it's not as if it's a big secret." She hesitated. "But I'd appreciate it if you didn't spread it around."

"Of course," Maddie promised.

Suzanne nodded.

"I'd just graduated high school, and I was in love with my boyfriend, Richard. We were pretty serious – or so I thought." She sighed. "My family was well off." She gestured to the house behind them. "We lived here back then – in fact, my grandfather built it – and I was happy here. My father was strict, but I thought he loved me." She laughed bitterly.

"What happened?" Suzanne asked.

"He caught us together one day." She smiled wryly at their surprised expressions. "Not like *that*. We'd decided to wait a little longer. But my father caught us kissing in the garage—" she gestured to the coach house next to the house "—and assumed the worst. I didn't know he was such a snob." She shook her head.

"Mrrow?"

"Richard was from the wrong side of the tracks, dear," she told Trixie. "He was a good person – a great person – and he couldn't help being poor. His parents

161

were hard workers, but they could only get badly paid jobs, so they couldn't get ahead. He was about to start work in a couple of weeks at the mill so we were enjoying our time together until then. In the fall I was supposed to go to college."

"What happened?" Now it was Maddie's turn to ask.

"My father threatened him with his handgun. He must have spotted us, gone back to his study and retrieved his gun. Said he'd shoot him if he saw us together again. I pleaded with Dad, but he wouldn't listen." She shook her head in regret. "I never saw Richard again."

"You didn't?" Suzanne looked shocked. "Couldn't you arrange to meet him secretly?"

"I wanted to," Grace told her. "But I couldn't chance being seen going to his house. Back then there weren't cell phones or the internet. I couldn't risk calling him on the landline inside the house, and his parents didn't have a telephone back then."

"Wow," Suzanne murmured.

"I begged my father to continue to let me see Richard, but he wouldn't listen. And then …"

"Yes?" Maddie was eager to hear more.

"I heard he'd left town with Veronica," Grace said in a rush.

"What?" Suzanne looked shocked.

"It was two weeks after my father threatened him. My friend told me. Later, I heard that they'd gotten married and were living in Idaho. I thought he loved me." The older woman seemed to blink back tears.

"I'm so sorry," Maddie said. She couldn't imagine that happening to her and Luke.

"I thought Veronica got a college scholarship," Suzanne said, looking puzzled.

"She did." Grace nodded. "I heard she went to college and Richard got a job in the same town and they were married for years."

"Oh." Maddie's heart went out to Grace.

"Mrrow," Trixie said softly.

"So you can see why I disliked that woman." Grace straightened her spine.

"You didn't meet anyone else?" Suzanne asked delicately.

"No." Grace shook her head. "My father was determined I marry well, but none of the men he introduced me to appealed to me. Even guys I met through the normal way ..." she sighed "It just wasn't the same. What Richard and I had was special. Or I thought it was. I didn't want to "settle" so I didn't marry anyone."

"What about your father?" Maddie couldn't help asking.

"He didn't like it, but apart from dragging me to the altar, there wasn't anything he could do about it. I finally told him I would never marry since he ruined my chance with Richard." She shrugged. "By that time, he'd mellowed a little, and said he regretted what he'd done, but by then it was too late. As far as I knew Richard was still married to Veronica."

"When was that?" Suzanne asked.

"About ten years ago," Grace said. "My father died not long after, and left me everything."

"But Veronica seemed to be on her own when she returned to Estherville." Suzanne tapped her lips.

"I know." Grace nodded. "That struck me as odd because I was sure she'd love to parade the fact she'd stolen Richard from me and that they were still together."

"No one's said anything to you about him?" Maddie asked delicately.

"No. And none of my friends know, either."

"That *is* strange," Suzanne said.

Grace nodded, then checked her watch.

"Oh dear, is that the time? You girls will have to excuse me. I've got a church meeting in half an hour."

"Of course," Maddie said.

"Thanks for the cuttings." Suzanne waved the paper bag. "I'll go home and plant them."

They said goodbye and got into Maddie's car.

"Wow!" Suzanne buckled up. "I'm glad my family isn't like Grace's. Nothing is going to stop me from seeing Ramon."

"Not even a gun pointed at you?" Maddie started the engine.

"Nope." Suzanne's ponytail swished. "Surely there was a way they could have sent messages to each other and made plans to run away together," she mused.

"Maybe it's harder to organize that in real life than it is in the movies and books," Maddie replied. "They didn't have email back then, either."

"I have no idea how people managed in the old days." Suzanne shuddered dramatically.

Maddie smiled as they drove back to the town square, then sobered. She'd been moved by Grace's story and had felt sorry for the older woman. She just hoped it wasn't an omen for her and Luke or Suzanne and Ramon.

CHAPTER 16

"So now we have to ask Pamela some questions," Suzanne said when they arrived back at Brewed from the Bean. It was just after 3.30.

Maddie took down the sign and opened the serving hatch. Since they were due to close in thirty minutes it seemed a little silly to open for business again, but time and again someone had been desperate for an afternoon caffeine fix.

"Poor Grace." Maddie stroked Trixie's plush fur as the feline sat on the stool. She counted herself lucky to have Trixie, her parents, Suzanne, and now Luke, in her life.

"Her father sounded like a real jerk." Suzanne frowned. "*I* wouldn't have let anyone stop me from seeing Richard."

"Even if it meant you were putting his life in danger by defying your father's orders?" Maddie asked.

"Surely her father wouldn't have shot Richard," Suzanne argued. "If he did, then he'd go to jail."

"I'd like to think that," Maddie said slowly. "But Grace's family must have been a big deal in town. He could have said his gun went off by accident. No one would want to believe a pillar of the community could do such a thing."

Although she wasn't in Grace's circle of friends, one reason being the woman was over twenty years older than her, Maddie had heard of Grace's family from time to time as she grew up. They were well respected, and one of the richer families in Estherville – if not the wealthiest. Grace's father could have all sorts of connections with the sheriff's department and the local judge, especially back then.

"I hate that you might be right," Suzanne grumbled.

"Mrrow," Trixie seemed to agree.

Maddie looked at her watch. No customers and five minutes until closing.

"Why don't we come up with a plan to bump into Pamela?" she suggested. "Veronica stole her chance of being a cheerleader."

"Just what I was going to say." Suzanne smiled at her as she pulled out her phone from her pocket. "Now, let's see. How often does she stop by for coffee?"

"Once or twice per week," Maddie replied.

"I haven't seen her since before Veronica's murder, have you?" Suzanne asked.

"No." Maddie's eyes rounded as she stared at her friend.

"You don't think—" they said in unison.

"Just because she hasn't come by the truck in a few days doesn't mean she's the killer." Suzanne's words were sensible but her tone was anything but. Her eyes sparkled with excitement.

"That's right." Maddie nodded.

"We've got to talk to her!" Suzanne closed the serving hatch. "No customers. And right now, this is way more important!"

"Mrrow!"

"I see Trixie agrees with you," Maddie said wryly, glancing affectionately at her familiar.

"Mrrow!"

"Pamela works at the bank, doesn't she?" Suzanne looked thoughtful.

"Yes." Maddie nodded. "Part-time, I think."

"Perfect!" Suzanne snapped her fingers. "Tomorrow we can go in and talk to her."

"And hold up a line of customers behind us?" Maddie asked skeptically. "Besides, do you really think she's going to tell us anything in a room full of co-workers and customers?"

"You're right." Suzanne's expression fell. "But how are we going to get her alone?"

"Mrrow!" Trixie said urgently. She stared intently at Maddie. An image slowly rose in Maddie's mind of giving Pamela a special coupon for a free coffee from their truck.

Maddie blinked, then smiled at Trixie. "Did you do that, Trix?"

The familiar seemed to nod.

"What? What have I missed?" Suzanne demanded, her gaze swiveling from Maddie to Trixie and back again.

"Trixie has just given me an idea," Maddie replied, marveling once more at her cat's magical abilities.

"How?" Suzanne's eyes widened. "You mean by telepathy? Like when you two spoke to each other when we were in Seattle and Trixie was here?"

"Yep." Maddie nodded. "And I think her idea will work."

***

That evening, Maddie and Suzanne printed out a coupon they'd created on the computer.

For our special customers only – one free coffee of your choice, including our popular iced coffees and whipped cream specials.

It had been Suzanne's idea to mention the specials.

"That should do it," Suzanne said smugly as they stared at the brown and white token, designed to match the coffee bean decoration on their truck. "No one can resist a free drink. And when she claims it, we'll pounce on her and ask her some probing questions."

"Mrrow!"

"Don't get too carried away," Maddie cautioned. "Pamela could be totally innocent."

"But she's our last suspect," Suzanne said. "We haven't heard about anyone else having a beef with Veronica – although I'm sure there are plenty who have in the past."

"Maybe Detective Edgewater has some leads," Maddie suggested.

"I hope so." Suzanne took the coupon and tucked it in her purse. "I'll drop this in to Pamela as soon as the bank is open."

"Okay." Maddie nodded. "Then come straight back to the truck. If we get a rush of customers in the morning, I'll need your help."

"Gotcha."

***

The next morning, Suzanne left Brewed from the Bean at nine o'clock, and came back in a few minutes, her face flushed.

"I did it!"

"Good!" Maddie heaped foamed milk on top of a cappuccino, sprinkled chocolate powder on top, and handed it to her sixty-something customer. "There you are, Mrs. Lowell."

"Thank you, dear." The petite woman took a tiny sip. "Delicious as always, Maddie."

Suzanne waited until their customer left. "Pamela said she'd stop by today after work. She finishes at three-thirty."

"Okay," Maddie replied with a smile before their regular customers kept them busy for the rest of the morning.

"I've been thinking," Maddie said, when she got a chance to sit down and rest her feet. She unwrapped her turkey sandwich. "We should find out more about Richard."

"Veronica's missing husband! Of course!" Plastic wrap rustled as Suzanne unwrapped her own sandwich. Today she was indulging in peanut butter and raisins. "Thood idea," she mumbled through a gooey mouthful.

Trixie had just finished eating her own lunch of sardines in spring water, and now sat up on her stool, giving them her full attention.

"Mrrow."

"I think it's really strange he didn't come back to town with Veronica." Suzanne pondered after she'd swallowed a bite. "Unless he was too embarrassed to run into Grace?"

"After thirty-two years?" Maddie frowned.

"But what if she was his one true love and he blew it by running off with Veronica?" Suzanne suggested. "He couldn't face her again! So he stayed home – wherever that is – while Veronica came back here to visit Claudine."

"Hmm." Maddie nibbled on her sandwich.

"Or," Suzanne paused dramatically, "he's the killer!"

"What?" Maddie put down her sandwich and stared at her friend.

"Mrrow?"

"Just think about it," Suzanne urged. "He made a big mistake marrying Veronica. She's driving him crazy and he can't take it anymore. So he sneaks into Estherville, kills her, and sneaks home.

No one would suspect him, because Veronica hasn't even mentioned him during her visit. Plus, all the stuff that happened with him and Grace was thirty-two years ago. There mightn't be many people around now who lived here back then. I don't think Detective Edgewater was here, for example."

"Good point," Maddie conceded.

"Mrrow." Trixie sounded approving.

"But wouldn't Detective Edgewater already be looking into this? He would know if Veronica was still married to Richard, wouldn't he? Next of kin and all that kind of thing?"

"You're right." Suzanne looked a little deflated. "I bet Claudine would know but there's no way I'm asking her."

"Me neither."

"Mrrow!" Trixie agreed.

"Next time we see Detective Edgewater we could ask him," Maddie proposed.

"Definitely!" Suzanne munched on her sandwich. "Ath thoon ath I finith thith—" she waved her sandwich in the air "—I'll make a note on our thuthpect litht."

"I wonder if Pamela knows anything about it?" Maddie mused. "We should find a way to ask her."

"Yeth!" Suzanne swallowed her mouthful and took a gulp of water. "I just hope she stops by when there aren't any other customers."

Suzanne's wish was granted. Just after three-thirty, Pamela appeared at the counter, holding the coupon Suzanne had given her that morning.

"It's so nice of you girls to give me this freebie," she said, a smile on her face. "I love your coffee, Maddie. I'm so glad you set up your truck here."

"Thanks, Pamela." Maddie smiled at the trim fiftyish woman.

"Only our very special customers received one of these coupons," Suzanne told her, not seeming to have an issue that Pamela had been the only recipient. "What would you like?"

"I'd love to try an iced coffee. My friends have been raving about them." Pamela's eyes lit up.

"Coming right up." Maddie set to work, the machine grinding and hissing.

"And next time you'll have to try our new iced mocha," Suzanne said.

"You girls are too much!" Pamela grinned.

Suzanne made a point of squirting a huge mound of whipped cream on top of the icy beverage.

"Oh, Suzanne!" Pamela's eyes widened. "You're going to make me fat!"

"Nonsense," Suzanne replied. "You're very slim."

"I do try to keep active," Pamela replied, "although I don't think I could get up at six to go jogging before work."

"Who could?" Suzanne shuddered.

Maddie could almost see the moment that Suzanne had thought of how to lead into asking about Veronica.

"Did you pursue cheerleading after high school?" Suzanne asked.

"No." Pamela shook her head. "I went to college, but since I hadn't had any high school experience, I figured I wouldn't pass the auditions. And what if somehow word had reached them from Estherville High about how I was accused of stealing a cheer? I decided I wanted a fresh start at college, so that meant not having anything to do with cheering." Regret flickered across her face.

"That's a shame," Maddie said sympathetically.

"Mrrow."

"It's okay, Trixie," Pamela told the Persian. "I've had a pretty good life. I like living here and my job at the bank suits me. And I have friends. They know I would never steal anything. And some of them have had problems with Veronica as well."

"Really?" Suzanne asked.

"Amy and Grace." Pamela nodded. "We were all at high school together."

Maddie and Suzanne exchanged a glance. So far, they hadn't learned anything new but …

"I heard Veronica had a husband," Suzanne began.

Pamela's face clouded. "You mean she stole him."

"Was he—" Maddie began carefully. She didn't want to betray Grace's confidence, but before she could worry about it, Pamela helped her out.

"She stole him from Grace." Pamela took a big sip of her cream covered drink and sighed in satisfaction. "Now I know what my friends have been raving about. Mm."

"Glad you like it." Suzanne smiled. "But do you know why Veronica didn't bring her husband with her to Estherville?"

"No idea." Pamela shook her head. "No one had heard about them for years and years. I often wondered when Grace went off to college – a different one – if she would return with Richard. She could have hired a private investigator and tracked him down – but when I asked her one day if she'd done that, she'd said no. Even though her family was wealthy, her father didn't give her a lot of spending money while she was at school." She laughed mirthlessly. "Maybe he was afraid she would do that very thing."

"So you never heard about Richard again?" Maddie asked curiously.

"No. Only that he and Veronica got married and were living in Idaho. That's all."

"Huh." Suzanne looked thoughtful.

"I heard you were the one who found Veronica's body." Pamela patted Suzanne's shoulder. "You poor thing."

"Thanks. It's something that I hope doesn't happen again," Suzanne replied soberly.

"Does the sheriff's department have any news?" Pamela asked.

"If they do, they haven't told us." Suzanne shook her head.

"That's too bad." Pamela took another slurp of her drink. "Although I think murder is a terrible thing, I also hope – sort of – that the killer gets away with it. I'm sure they had a very good reason for killing Veronica, and to be honest, I don't think anyone will mourn her – apart from Claudine and Richard."

CHAPTER 17

"That was a bit of a bust." Suzanne's mouth drooped after Pamela left.

"Maybe this will cheer you up." Maddie waved an iced mocha in front of her friend's nose.

"Ooh!" Suzanne squirted cream on it, but not as much as she usually indulged in. "Thanks."

"We've learned that Richard's whereabouts are a bit of a mystery," Maddie said.

"Maybe he's run away!" Suzanne's eyes lit up. "Maybe he saw Veronica's trip here as his only chance to get away, so instead of killing her he tells her, "You go to Estherville, dear, and I'll stay home and look after things." And BAM!" Suzanne smacked her fist into her palm. "He runs off somewhere without leaving a trace – anywhere. He's an official ghost."

"I think you've been watching too much TV," Maddie said wryly.

"What do you think, Trix?" Suzanne turned to the feline. "Do you think I'm right, or do you think Maddie is?"

Trixie wrapped her fluffy silver tail around her white feet but didn't make a sound. She appeared to be thinking.

"Huh." Suzanne seemed disappointed.

"You can't be right all the time," Maddie teased.

"Can't I?" Suzanne made a moue, then sipped her drink, closing her eyes in appreciation.

"Maybe I should try the Tell the Truth spell," Maddie said slowly.

"Yes!" Suzanne's eyes flew open. "Honestly, Mads, I don't know why you don't use magic more often. We could solve our cases like that!" She snapped her fingers.

"You know I can only use the Tell the Truth spell once per full moon," Maddie reminded her. "And if I use it on the wrong person then we don't find out any new information."

"True," Suzanne said reluctantly. "But we could have used it on Pamela. Maybe there's something she's not telling us."

"I promise to use it on the next person we interview," Maddie said.

Suzanne pulled out her phone and frowned. "According to our list, we've spoken to all the suspects. Apart from the mysterious Richard, and the guy who was Luke's customer."

"And Luke told us that Detective Edgewater enquired about that man," Maddie reminded her.

"Yeah." Suzanne's tone was glum. "So what do we do now?"

"I guess we should find out more about Richard," Maddie replied. "And the best person to ask would be Detective Edgewater."

"So let's go and see him!" Suzanne jumped from the stool, looking ready to lock up the truck and go sleuthing.

"And say what? Give us all the information you have on Veronica's husband Richard?"

"It's a start!"

Before Maddie could reason with her, a looming figure at the counter snagged her attention.

"Detective Edgewater." Maddie smiled. "We were just talking about you."

"You're not psychic, are you?" Suzanne asked mischievously.

"No. Are you?" He peered at both of them.

"Nope."

"No," Maddie said. She didn't *think* she was. Apart from being able to do the Coffee Vision spell. Was being able to communicate telepathically with Trixie considered to be psychic? If she told anyone (apart from Suzanne) she didn't think they'd believe her. They might even laugh. A disquieting thought arose. Would Luke laugh?

Trixie didn't answer the detective's question.

"Your usual?" Suzanne's fingers were poised on the register.

"I thought I'd have another iced mocha."

"Good idea." Suzanne beamed at him. "I can put extra whipped cream on it for you."

"Maybe just a little bit – not as much as last time," he added hurriedly.

"No worries." Suzanne handed him his change.

"So," he said, tucking his wallet back into his pocket, "What were you two talking about – besides me?"

"We wondered if you knew about Veronica's husband," Suzanne said innocently.

"Yes, I do." He looked a trifle smug.

"Well?" Suzanne demanded.

"Do you really need to know?" he asked.

"Yes!"

"Suzanne," Maddie hissed. They had to remember that however genial the detective seemed to be – most of the time – he was still a law enforcement officer. Sometimes Suzanne's curiosity got the better of her.

"It's a matter of public record," he told Maddie. "Richard Darin died a while ago. Cancer."

"Oh." Maddie didn't know what to say.

"So that's why Veronica came back to Estherville on her own," Suzanne said.

"It looks that way," Detective Edgewater agreed.

Suzanne squirted a small amount of cream on his drink.

"More?" she asked.

"No. That looks perfect."

Suzanne handed him the drink, looking doubtful at his pronouncement.

"What other info do you have?" Suzanne asked.

"We're making good progress with the case," he told her.

"And you spoke to the guy who was in my brother Luke's shop? The one who grumbled about Veronica?" Suzanne pressed.

"Yes."

Maddie thought he refrained from rolling his eyes.

"We do know what we're doing." He sipped his drink, as if trying to stave off any more questions. "Delicious, Maddie." He smiled at her.

"Thanks," she replied.

"How are you, Trixie?" He glanced over at the Persian.

"Mrrow," she said, as if she were deep in thought.

"She's been pretty quiet all day," Maddie said.

"She's thinking," Suzanne declared.

Detective Edgewater chuckled. "You'll keep an eye on these two, won't you, Trixie?"

"Mrrow!" Trixie opened her turquoise eyes wide and stared at him, as if to say, *"I already am."*

CHAPTER 18

"We should go over the facts of the case," Suzanne said that evening. They sat at Maddie's pine kitchen table, each sipping on a latte.

"Mrrow!" Trixie seemed to nod her head. She sat on "her" chair at the table.

"Okay." Maddie glanced at Suzanne's phone where she'd written down the information about the murder. "Veronica was killed by a heavy object."

"Hmm." Suzanne tapped her fingernails on the table. "Like a big rock or—"

"Maybe the lid of the garbage can?" Maddie suggested.

"Yes! Eww." Suzanne sank back in her chair. "What if I touched the murder weapon when I lifted the garbage can lid to see what was inside?" She shook off the thought.

"Maybe the lid wasn't heavy enough." Maddie was sorry she thought of the notion. "Besides, it can't have been that because Detective Edgewater didn't ask for your fingerprints, did he?"

"No." Suzanne brightened. "Good. She wasn't killed by a metal garbage lid."

There was silence for a few seconds.

"So what did kill her?" Suzanne looked stumped.

Maddie looked at Trixie, raising her eyebrow in inquiry. But her familiar didn't say anything at all.

"Maybe we should leave that question to one side right now," Maddie proposed. "Is there anyone else we need to interview?"

Suzanne glanced down at her phone. "No." She sighed. "And now we know what happened with the mysterious Richard – so he couldn't have killed Veronica. Poor Grace."

"Do you think she knows he … passed away?" Maddie asked.

"I don't know." Suzanne looked thoughtful. "It didn't sound like she did when she spoke about him breaking her heart, but who knows?"

"And I don't want to have to ask her if she *did* know," Maddie said.

"Exactly," Suzanne agreed. "I'll just make a note here next to Grace's name – *not sure if she knows Richard dead.*"

"What about Claudine?" Maddie said reluctantly. "Do you think she could have—"

"Yes!" Suzanne jumped up and paced in front of Maddie. "It makes perfect sense that Claudine is the killer!"

"Maybe because you want it to be so," Maddie said gently. She didn't like Claudine, but had she actually murdered her cousin? She'd genuinely seemed upset by Veronica's death.

"Don't you?" Suzanne demanded.

"Not really." Maddie shook her head. "I thought I should mention the possibility but it would mean that Claudine is even scarier than we thought. Other than the argument she had with Veronica over their coffee stand—"

"*Illegal* coffee stand."

"—she seems to have liked Veronica."

"Hmm." Suzanne pondered. "I hate to say this, but I think you might be right."

"Gee, thanks," Maddie replied.

"But I still think we should question her just to make sure."

"Okay," Maddie said reluctantly. She'd love *not* to have to talk to Claudine.

After another moment of silence, Maddie said, "I guess I'll have to use the Tell the Truth spell next time."

"Do you have it ready?" Suzanne asked.

"In my pocket." Maddie patted her shorts' pocket.

"What about the incantation from the night of the full moon?" Suzanne inquired. "When are you going to use that?"

"When we need to find where someone is," Maddie replied. "Maybe someone on our list that we need to question?"

"Cool!"

Suzanne's ring tone sounded a jazzy tune. She looked at the phone curiously before she picked it up.

"It's Ramon!" Suzanne looked like she couldn't decide whether to grin or pass out.

Maddie gestured for her to take the call.

Suzanne picked up her phone, faced Maddie and Trixie, hesitated, then got up and walked over to the kitchen sink, turning her back to them.

Maddie glanced at Trixie. The Persian seemed to be smiling.

"Hi Ramon." Suzanne used her "boyfriend" voice. The one that seemed to say to the caller, I may be bouncy and cheerful, but I'm also feminine and girly. Maddie hadn't heard her use it in a while.

"I'd love to."

Maddie tried not to overhear, but it was impossible to resist temptation. If she truly did not want to listen, she'd have to leave the room.

After a couple of minutes of Suzanne continuing to use her "boyfriend" voice, she ended the call, a big smile on her face.

"Ramon asked me out – to dinner!"

"That's great!" Maddie smiled back at her friend.

"Mrrow!" Trixie sounded pleased.

"Oh, Mads, he's taking me to this little Italian restaurant he's found in a nearby town. And he's picking me up!"

"Awesome!"

They high-fived, then Suzanne held her hand out to Trixie. The Persian put her paw out, and Suzanne gently high-fived the cat.

"Mrrow!"

"When?" Maddie asked.

"Friday night." Suzanne's eyes grew dreamy, then she jerked to attention. "Oh no! How on earth am I going to decide what to wear? And what about my hair?" She pulled at her ponytail.

"Why don't you do your hair the same way you did for your first lunch date with him?"

"Good idea." Suzanne looked a little relieved. "But you'll have to help me choose an outfit – something that makes me look good, but not something that sends the wrong message, *if you know what I mean.*"

"What message would that be?" Maddie couldn't help teasing.

"Oh, you!" Suzanne mimed throwing a cushion at her.

They both laughed, Trixie looking from one to the other as if she didn't understand why they found their conversation so funny.

"Of course I'll come over," Maddie said, as soon as she got enough breath back to speak. "Trixie, do you want to go to Suzanne's house with me? We'll help her choose an outfit for her date with Ramon."

"Mrrow!" Trixie seemed to nod.

"Good." Suzanne smiled. "You never know, maybe Trixie will choose the perfect dress for me."

***

Maddie had her own date with Luke on Friday night, but all through the movie she couldn't help but wonder how Suzanne's dinner date with Ramon was going. Last night, she and Trixie went to Suzanne's house after they closed up Brewed from the Bean and went through Suzanne's entire wardrobe.

Suzanne had shaken her head at most of the outfits Maddie had suggested. It was only when Trixie had gently touched a lavender frock with her paw that Suzanne had brightened and declared it the obvious choice.

Maddie hoped her bestie's evening went well. She wasn't sure if she *didn't* hear from Suzanne tonight if that meant the date was still going on, or if it had been a bust.

With a start, she realized she and Suzanne had been so busy anticipating her date with Ramon that they hadn't done anything about re-interviewing anyone on their suspect list.

"Are you cold?" Luke whispered to Maddie in the darkened air-conditioned theater, as he placed his arm around her shoulder.

His warmth instantly made her feel better.

"Thanks," she murmured, trying to return her attention to the movie, and not on the shiver of pleasure at his touch, or the fact that Suzanne would most likely be devastated if her evening with Ramon didn't go well.

After the movie, Luke took her home. Trixie waited at the door for them and scampered ahead of them to the kitchen. After Maddie made lattes, they cuddled on the couch for a while, Trixie letting them have a little time alone.

Maddie had kept her phone turned off all evening – Suzanne had assured her she wouldn't need to call her during her date with Ramon.

When Luke left, after giving her a goodnight kiss that left *her* feeling totally feminine and girly, Maddie turned on her phone. No missed calls or texts. She hoped it was a good omen.

***

Bang! Bang! Bang!

"Wake up!" she heard a faint cry.

Maddie's phone sounded with its old-fashioned ring tone on the nightstand.

Maddie woke up with a jerk.

"Whaaa?" She rubbed the sleep out of her eyes.

Trixie stood on the vacant side of the bed, looking at Maddie's phone with wide eyes. She had never seemed to like the noise it made when someone called, even after Maddie had tried every ring tone she could think of to please the Persian.

Maddie grabbed the phone and answered it.

"I've got to talk to you!" Suzanne shrieked at the other end.

"Where are you?" Maddie became alert.

"At your front door. Didn't you hear me calling out to you to wake up?"

"Okay." Maddie hopped out of bed and jogged down the hall. She couldn't tell if Suzanne was happy or upset.

She opened the door to a bright and sunny day – and an ecstatic looking Suzanne.

"He kissed me!"

"Come in." Maddie smiled, wondering if Suzanne's scream had awakened the whole street.

"Oh, Mads! I couldn't wait any longer to tell you!"

Maddie led the way into the kitchen, happiness bursting in her heart for her friend. Trixie appeared at her heels.

"Trix, you were right about the dress." Suzanne giggled.

"Mrrow!"

"Tell me everything," Maddie urged.

"I'm desperate for a coffee." Suzanne looked hopefully at the machine on the kitchen counter.

"I am too." Maddie was suddenly conscious of being in her knee length t-shirt nightgown while Suzanne was dressed in a blue t-shirt and denim shorts. "What's the time?"

"Six-thirty, but I couldn't wait any longer to see you!" Suzanne sat down at the kitchen table, then jumped up and paced the room.

"Oh, Mads, it was wonderful! The Italian restaurant was amazing! Everything tasted so good! And there weren't many people there, so it felt like we had the whole place to ourselves."

"Mmm." Maddie smiled as she turned on the espresso machine.

"I had mushroom risotto and he had pasta primavera, but you should have seen the way he looked at me, Mads. You know I like eating, but for once I found it difficult because my stomach was so churned up inside, but in a good way."

Wow. Suzanne definitely had feelings for Ramon. She didn't rave about many of her dates – not like this.

"Mrrow?" Trixie asked.

"And then we talked and talked, Trix. It was wonderful!" Suzanne stopped pacing and stroked the Persian. "And Ramon told me ..." she trailed off.

Maddie turned from the machine to look at her. "What did he tell you? If you want to tell me – us," she amended as she glanced at Trixie, who looked just as curious as Maddie felt. "It's okay if you want to keep it to yourself," she added, remembering how Luke had made her feel last night – all girly and feminine.

"He said – he said—" Suzanne giggled, her face going bright red. "He said he thinks I'm amazing, Mads!" She twirled around.

"Of course you are."

"But he's the amazing one," Suzanne told her. "He can speak three languages, Italian as well as Spanish and English, and you know what an incredible masseur he is – well, no you don't, because even though I've told you to go and get a massage with him, you haven't, but never mind about that now. And he said …" her voice trailed off again.

"What?" Maddie couldn't help wanting to know.

"He was a little worried about the age difference," Suzanne rushed out. "I told him I wasn't. That some of the guys my age are *so immature* and still live at home with their parents—" the expression on her face indicated that was one of the worst crimes in the world "—and that I haven't been dating much lately because I just haven't felt attracted to anyone – until I met him." She giggled. "And I think he blushed – just a tiny bit! Can you believe that?"

Maddie shook her head. She didn't think she could. She handed a latte to Suzanne.

"Drink this."

"Thanks." Suzanne took a big gulp. "Perfect as always." She sighed in pleasure.

"Then what happened?" Maddie asked. "If I'm allowed to ask."

"Of course you are!" Suzanne waved the latte in the air, nearly spilling it. "That's why I'm here! To tell you all about it!"

She took another sip of her coffee. "So, after dinner, we went to this art gallery nearby, and looked at some of the paintings. Honestly, Mads, I don't understand modern art. I think I could scribble something on a canvas with crayon and that gallery would show it for me."

"I know what you mean," Maddie replied, thinking of the times she'd ventured into the modern art section of a museum.

"Anyway, it was just an excuse to spend more time together," Suzanne said, sitting back down at the table. "Then he drove me home and—" she drew in a deep breath.

"And?" Maddie held her own breath.

"Mrrow?" Trixie's eyes were rounded as she waited for Suzanne to continue.

"He came inside and checked the house for me! To make sure it was safe for me! Isn't that so … so … chivalrous?"

"Yes, it is," Maddie replied seriously.

"Mrrow." Trixie seemed to nod.

"And then – he kissed me! In the hall! Before he left!"

Maddie felt like shouting, "Yay!" but settled for a big smile.

"It was wonderful. He really knows what he's doing." Suzanne sighed, her expression dreamy.

"When are you seeing him again?" Maddie asked, hoping she wasn't asking the wrong question.

"Tomorrow!" Suzanne laughed with delight. "He's taking me on a picnic! Isn't that romantic?"

"Yes," Maddie replied truthfully. She'd thought her recent picnic with Luke was romantic, maybe even more so because he'd welcomed Trixie along as well.

Suzanne giggled. "It's the same park you and my brother went to. But there isn't anywhere else around where we could sit and relax and just enjoy each other's company – unless it's at my house."

"Or his," Maddie said mischievously.

"One day." Suzanne's eyes sparkled. "I hope."

Maddie rushed to get ready so they could open Brewed from the Bean on time that morning. Suzanne kept chatting to her, following Maddie from room to room, enthusing about Ramon.

By the time they arrived at the town square, Suzanne finally seemed to run out of breath.

Maddie was happy for her friend – more than happy. Her friend deserved to have the boyfriend of her dreams.

CHAPTER 19

"As soon as we close at lunchtime, we should visit Claudine," Suzanne told her as Maddie flopped down on a stool. They'd just finished serving a stream of customers.

"I guess," Maddie replied reluctantly.

"Have you got the Tell the Truth spell?"

"In my pocket." Maddie patted her shorts.

"Maybe it's just as well Trixie stayed home this morning," Suzanne said.

"Definitely. She doesn't like Claudine."

"Who could blame her?" Suzanne sympathized.

Maddie tried to keep her mind off their upcoming visit. She wished she could leave Suzanne to do the questioning, but the spell only seemed to work if she was the one who used it.

Since they opened for mornings only on Saturday, at lunchtime they locked up and walked over to the café. Once they interviewed Claudine, they'd hop in the truck and drive it back to Maddie's house.

"Maybe this isn't the right time," Maddie said as they neared Claudine's coffee shop. "She might be slammed with customers."

"I don't think that's ever happened." Suzanne's ponytail swished in emphasis.

They stood outside the front door and stared at each other.

"Together," Suzanne said.

Maddie nodded as she and her friend placed their hands on the door and pushed at the same time.

There were only two customers inside – an elderly man sipping a hot drink and a big burly man reading a newspaper. Maddie felt better that they weren't interrupting Claudine during a busy time.

"What are you doing here?" Claudine appeared from the rear of the shop. Her voice was a growl.

"We wanted to say we were sorry about your cousin," Maddie said.

"You said that before," Claudine informed her.

Suzanne tilted her head toward Maddie as if to say, *"Use the truth spell."*

Maddie fingered her pocket. During one of their quiet periods that morning she'd memorized the words.

Maddie took a deep breath and looked around, not wanting anyone else to hear their conversation. Luckily, there wasn't anyone near them. Claudine seemed to be the only worker in the shop.

She silently uttered the words, seeing them in her mind, and whispering, "Show me," at the end.

"Did you know about Veronica's husband? Richard?" She looked directly at Claudine.

"Yeah. So what?" Claudine shrugged.

It was working! Somehow, Maddie knew deep inside that Claudine told the truth.

"That he died?" Suzanne put in.

Maddie sent her a warning look.

Suzanne mimed a *Sorry!*

"Yes. Why do you want to know?" Claudine snapped.

"We were wondering who had a motive to kill Veronica," Maddie told her.

"I still think it was you two." Claudine glared at them.

Maddie didn't think *that* was the truth.

"Who else?" she probed.

Claudine shrugged. "I don't know. Veronica was a great person. She used to let me tag along with her sometimes before she left Estherville. That was when I was young, and she was a teenager. She didn't have to do that." She swiped her eye.

Maddie nodded, then looked at Suzanne. She couldn't very well ask the woman if she killed Veronica, could she?

"Since you're here, you can give me my plant pot back," Claudine demanded.

"What?" Suzanne wrinkled her forehead.

"You know what I'm talking about."

"No, we don't," Maddie told Claudine.

"The old plant pot I put in the garbage can. Before *the killer* stuffed Veronica's body in there." She looked at the two of them as if she still believed they'd murdered Veronica, but Maddie knew better, thanks to the Tell the Truth spell.

"What are you talking about?" Suzanne asked in exasperation.

"Someone stole my pot!"

"But I thought you said you put it in the trash," Maddie said.

"I did because I'd chipped it on the side which ruined its look, but then I had second thoughts about finally getting rid of it. I haven't been able to find another one like it, with the blue and white marbling. After they ... found Veronica, I asked about the plant pot because I wanted it back, but law enforcement said there wasn't anything else in that can. Since you were lurking in the alley—" Claudine glared at them "—you must have taken it."

Suzanne recoiled. "You think we touched Veronica's body – actually moved it – in order to steal an old plant pot?" She looked at Claudine as if she were crazy.

"Who else would have taken it?" Claudine put her hands on her stout hips. "It was the only thing in that trash can the night before. *You* found Veronica. And now the plant pot is missing!"

"Why are you only asking us about it now?" Suzanne narrowed her eyes.

"Because I was too upset to focus before," Claudine snapped. *"My cousin was murdered."*

"We didn't take your pot," Maddie assured Claudine. "Suzanne didn't see it when she lifted the – lid. Did you?" She turned to her friend.

"No." Suzanne's ponytail bounced from side to side. "I didn't see anything apart from—" she swallowed hard.

"We *are* sorry about Veronica," Maddie told her nemesis.

"Yes." Suzanne sounded sincere.

"I've got work to do." Claudine stalked to the counter and stood behind the register. "If you're not going to buy anything, you can leave."

"Fine." Suzanne drew herself up to her full height of five foot six and strode out of the shop.

Maddie followed her friend.

"Wow!" Suzanne fumed as they hit the sidewalk. "I can't believe her." She turned around to Maddie. "So? What did the spell tell you?"

"She was telling the truth apart from when she said we were the killers," Maddie replied.

"Ha! So she doesn't think we murdered Veronica."

"Not really."

"But that's weird about how she's suddenly talking about this plant pot. I honestly didn't see anything else in …" she trailed off.

"It's okay." Maddie touched her arm. "Maybe not think about that moment."

"Good idea." Suzanne swallowed.

Something jiggled in Maddie's mind, but she didn't know what. Something about the plant pot. What was it? If Trixie were here, maybe she would know and they could work it out together. She'd have to ask her familiar.

"Let's go home," Maddie suggested.

"Good idea." Suzanne smiled. "Don't forget, I've got to get ready for my picnic with Ramon tomorrow."

"As if I could," Maddie teased. She had her own date tonight – Luke was coming over and she was cooking dinner for him. Something easy so she wouldn't get frazzled in the kitchen, but also impressive and delicious, like teriyaki chicken.

They'd reached Brewed from the Bean and were about to hop in and drive back to Maddie's when Grace hurried over to them.

"You girls aren't closed, are you?"

"Yes," Maddie said. "But I can make you something if you're desperate."

"I am." Grace sighed. "My own machine acted up this morning and I didn't have any instant in the house. I've had to *go without*."

"That's terrible!" Suzanne tsked. "I don't think I could bear it if I missed a day of caffeine."

Maddie jumped into the back of the truck and turned on the espresso machine. As she waited for it to warm up, she half-tuned in to Suzanne and Grace's conversation.

"How are your honeysuckle cuttings coming along?" Grace asked.

"Fine." Suzanne smiled. "I've put them in their own little pots and I think they're growing! Well, they seem okay, anyway."

"That's good," Grace told her. "You girls are welcome to come and look at my garden anytime. I love spending time in it and trying out different plants."

Maddie suddenly inhaled. Her mind flashed to an image of the blue and white marbled plant pot in Grace's garden.

She looked at Grace with widened eyes, then bent her head to the espresso machine. She couldn't give anything away at this stage.

Her mind worked furiously as she made Grace's latte. How on earth could the older woman be the killer? How could she have murdered Veronica?

Maybe there was another plant pot with the same pattern. It might not be Claudine's missing pot, she reasoned with herself. Maybe Grace had bought the rest of the pots like that and that's why Claudine couldn't buy another one to replace the chipped one.

Feeling slightly better, she handed Grace the latte.

"Thanks girls." Grace sipped her coffee and made a sound of appreciation.

"Just what I needed." She peered into the truck. "Where's Trixie?"

"She's having a day off." Maddie spoke lightly, still unable to believe that Grace might have killed Veronica.

"Give her a pat for me," Grace said.

"We will." Suzanne smiled as she closed up the register.

Maddie waited until Grace departed, then jumped into the driver's seat.

"What's the rush?" Suzanne wrinkled her nose. "You've still got plenty of time to cook my brother dinner."

"It's not that." Maddie started the engine. "Grace could be the killer!"

CHAPTER 20

"What?" Suzanne stared at Maddie as if she'd been drinking too much coffee. "No way!"

"Remember the plant pot Claudine was talking about?"

"How could I forget?"

"I saw one just like it in Grace's garden."

"You did? When we were there?"

"Yes." Maddie pulled into her driveway.

"Are you sure it was the same one?" Suzanne frowned.

"No, I'm not. I've been trying to tell myself that for the last few minutes. Maybe everyone in Estherville has the same pot with a chip in it."

"Do you think the local plant nursery would have a record of customers buying those pots – if they stock them?"

"I think we should call Detective Edgewater and tell him to check," Maddie replied.

"Good idea!"

They rushed inside Maddie's house. Trixie trotted to greet them, her ears pricking as she sensed what sort of mood they were in.

"Mrrow?"

"We need to call Detective Edgewater right away, Trix," Suzanne told the Persian.

"Mrrow!"

Maddie plucked her phone out of her pocket and dialed the number. After leaving a message for the detective, she sank down on a kitchen chair.

"I don't know what else to do," she confessed.

"I know what you mean." Suzanne drummed her fingers on her lips. "I can't believe Grace killed Veronica. I know we had her on our suspect list, and Veronica stole her high school boyfriend, but why would Grace kill her now? Especially since Richard has passed away."

"Exactly." Maddie nodded. "Maybe it isn't her." She sounded as if she were trying to convince herself. "Maybe everyone in Estherville does have the same kind of plant pot."

"With a chip in it?"

"Maybe it was a damaged shipment?" Maddie asked hopefully.

Maddie's phone rang. They looked at the flashing cell, then Maddie answered it.

"Detective Edgewater," she mouthed to Suzanne. After a moment, she said, "Okay, thank you," into the phone and finished the call. "He said he's going to check around Estherville this afternoon, since the plant nursery should still be open – and he'll ask Claudine where she bought the pot."

"Good." Suzanne sighed with relief. "Hopefully it means that Grace is in the clear."

A sudden thought struck Maddie and she groaned.

"What?" Suzanne peered at her.

"I've just remembered Claudine said *she* chipped the pot," Maddie said. "So that means—"

"It's not a damaged shipment," they spoke together.

"Oh pooh." Suzanne frowned. "I like Grace."

"So do I."

"Mrrow!" Trixie looked upset.

"Maybe there's a reasonable explanation for why Grace has the same kind of pot in her garden," Suzanne said. "Ooh!" She snapped her fingers. "Maybe the killer gave it to her!"

"Yes!" Maddie felt like cheering. "Surely that must be it?"

"We should go over to Grace's house and find out," Suzanne declared.

"Do you think that's wise?" Maddie asked, Detective Edgewater's words about not poking around in the investigation springing up in her mind.

"We should be safe because you can do magic!" Excitement flickered across Suzanne's face.

"But only a few spells," Maddie reminded her.

"Trixie can do a spell on her own, can't you, Trix?" Suzanne looked over at the familiar, who sat on "her" kitchen chair.

Maddie shuddered at the memory of the Freeze spell Trixie had cast to save her a few months ago.

"Mrrow!" Trixie said proudly, sitting up straight.

"I'm very grateful she did." Maddie stroked Trixie. "But I hope she doesn't have to repeat it."

"Hmm." Suzanne looked a little disappointed. "But we can still go and just talk to Grace, can't we?"

Maddie checked her watch. It was two-thirty.

"I guess we have time before Luke comes over this evening," she said reluctantly.

"Awesome! I know! You can use the new incantation to see where Grace is," Suzanne enthused.

"Sometimes I think you should be the witch," Maddie said wryly. But she knew if she ever lost what little powers she possessed, she'd definitely mourn the loss.

"I wish." Suzanne sighed.

"Let me get the incantation." Maddie rose from the table and headed to her bedroom. She'd placed the piece of paper that she'd written the spell on in her nightstand drawer.

A minute later, Maddie walked back into the kitchen.

"Okay." She placed the notepaper on the table. "It says I have to say these words in order to find somebody and see what they're doing right now."

Suzanne and Trixie were quiet while Maddie closed her eyes and focused. She opened her eyes and read out the words of the spell three times.

"Show me the person I am thinking of
Show me their actions
Show me true"

Maddie suddenly had a mental image of Grace. She was chatting to a friend at the library.

"Well?" Suzanne asked eagerly.

"She's at the library."

"Pooh." Suzanne pouted. "How can we talk privately to her there?"

Maddie closed her eyes and thought about Grace. Another image arose in her mind. Grace got in her car and drove in the direction of her house.

"I think she's going home," Maddie said, beginning to feel excited.

"You saw her twice?" Suzanne's eyes widened. "Can you see her again?"

Maddie shut her eyes and refocused, but this time nothing happened. No helpful image of Grace.

"No."

"So it looks like you get to use the spell twice in the first couple of minutes," Suzanne surmised. "Maybe you should cast it again!"

"Trixie?" Maddie looked to her familiar. "What do you think?" Sometimes she thought Trixie had a better handle on magic than she did.

"Mrrow!" Trixie seemed to nod her head.

"Okay." Maddie recited the words of the spell again. Another image of Grace. She was definitely driving in the direction of her house.

Maddie opened her eyes. "Let's go to Grace's house."

***

"Are we sure about this?" Maddie said doubtfully. They'd just pulled up to Grace's Victorian house.

"Of course." Suzanne sounded confident. "We're just going to talk to

her, that's all. We're not going to accuse
her of anything."

"That's good." Maddie looked at her
friend sideways. "Are you sure that's all
we're going to do?"

"Yes." Suzanne's ponytail swished.
"You show me where the pot is in her
garden and then I can ask her where she
got it from. I'll tell her I want to plant
some flower bulbs."

"Do you plant bulbs in summer?"
Maddie queried.

"Hmm." Suzanne whipped out her
phone and did a quick internet search.
"Apparently you plant spring flower
bulbs in the fall. If she asks, I'll just say I
love her pot so much I want one just like
it for next year's daffodils." Suzanne
looked satisfied with her reasoning.

"Okay." Maddie clipped on Trixie's
harness. "Let's go."

They opened the gate and walked into
Grace's garden.

"Over here," Maddie whispered,
discreetly pointing to a corner of the
garden filled with flowers. An empty blue
and white marbled pot stood next to a
border of pink dahlias.

"It does look nice." Suzanne bent down for a closer look, then suddenly recoiled as she remembered where the pot could have come from. "No wonder Claudine had second thoughts about getting rid of it."

"There's the chip." Maddie looked around but no one – including Grace – was in sight. A medium sized white chip ruined the decorative marbling on one side of the pot.

"Mrrow?" Trixie rubbed the side of her neck all around the pot, then pawed at the underside.

"What a shame." Suzanne straightened. "Because I would definitely want a pot like that if I didn't know it had been involved in a murder – somehow."

"Maybe we should check if Detective Edgewater's texted us," Maddie said hopefully.

"But you've had your phone on the whole time – haven't you?"

"Yes, but I might have put it on silent and not realized." Maddie dug the phone out of her pocket. No message or missed voice call from the detective. They were on their own.

They walked along Grace's path to the porch, Maddie hoping Grace wouldn't find it strange they were visiting her that afternoon.

"Trixie?" Maddie looked down at the Persian, but Trixie seemed intent on gazing at all the plants around them. If her familiar felt unsure about their plan, she wasn't showing it.

Suzanne pressed the doorbell, a loud chime echoing inside.

"Hi, girls." Grace seemed surprised to see them when she opened the door. "Oh, you've brought Trixie. How lovely!"

"Hi, Grace," Suzanne chirped. "Maddie and I were talking about the cuttings you gave me and I remembered I saw a really pretty pot in your garden that day. Did you buy it? Or did someone give it to you? I'd love to plant daffodil bulbs in something like that for next spring."

"Which pot, dear?" Grace asked. She gave a little laugh. "I do have lots in my garden."

"It has blue and white marbling." Suzanne pointed at the corner of the garden Maddie had shown her. "The pot

223

is empty at the moment," she added helpfully.

"Oh, that one."

Was it Maddie's imagination or had Grace paled just a little?

"I've had that pot for so long, I can't remember where I got it from. But maybe the local plant nursery has something similar."

"I'll check it out," Suzanne replied.

"Mrrow." Trixie put her paw on the doorstep and left something behind. A little speck of dark dried up stuff – was it soil?

"I'm so sorry," Maddie apologized. "Let me pick that up."

"No need." Grace bent down and scooped up the bit of dirt in her hand. "All gone."

"Mrrow!" Trixie sounded urgent as she looked at Maddie with widened eyes.

A speck of dark dirty – whatever it was. Maddie stared at her familiar when suddenly it clicked. The plant pot had been the murder weapon!

She straightened and turned to Grace, attempting to school her expression.

"You girls better come in." Grace held the door wide open for them.

"Thanks." Suzanne entered the house before Maddie could stop her.

"I think we should be going now," Maddie said, turning to leave. "We've got that *thing* on, Suzanne, remember?"

"What thing?" Suzanne swiveled around. "You mean you want to have plenty of time to get ready for Luke tonight. She's cooking dinner for my brother – eek!"

Grace had hauled Suzanne back into the house, a steely look of determination on her face.

"You know, don't you?" she snarled at Maddie.

"If you mean I know you killed Veronica, then yes," Maddie replied, her heart hammering in her chest.

"Mrrow!" Trixie agreed.

"Oh no," Suzanne groaned, attempting to wrestle her arm out of Grace's grasp. It was no use.

"If you want your friend to stay alive then you two better come in," Grace commanded.

Maddie looked down at Trixie. *I hope you've got a plan.* She just hoped the telepathic bond between them was working. Trixie's demeanor didn't give anything away.

"I won't allow you to hurt Suzanne," Maddie told Grace, using her most determined voice.

"Mrrow!"

"Then you better get inside." Grace narrowed her eyes at Maddie and Trixie, suddenly looking like a totally different person.

Once they were inside the hall, which was tastefully furnished with a mahogany antique dresser, Grace slammed the door shut behind them.

"We didn't want to believe you were the killer," Suzanne said.

"How did you know it was me?" Grace demanded.

"Claudine accused us of stealing her plant pot," Maddie told her.

"I knew I should have left that pot there." Grace screwed up her mouth in self-disgust. "But I couldn't resist it. I've never seen a pot like that and it was just thrown away like garbage. Just because it has a chip in it. Besides—" her shoulders sagged and she didn't seem quite as ferocious, "I thought it a good idea to remove it from the crime scene as it had my fingerprints all over it."

"So you used it to kill Veronica?" Maddie held her breath, waiting for confirmation.

"Yes." Grace nodded.

"But why?" Suzanne asked. "Why kill her?"

"She stole Richard," Grace replied. "And in doing so, she ruined my life."

"Did you know he died of cancer?" Maddie asked tentatively.

"Not until the day I murdered her," Grace replied, shuddering.

"What happened?" Maddie asked gently.

"I still don't know how it happened," Grace told them. "I was walking along the back alley as there's a wild piece of land nearby and I wanted to get a cutting of this unusual flower I saw there, when Veronica came out of the café's rear entrance. I didn't even want to say hello to her, but she said we should catch up.

Then she said she wanted to let me know Richard died of cancer two years ago!"

"Oh," Suzanne murmured.

"I couldn't believe it! I'd decided to swallow my pride and track him down, just before Veronica came to town, and when I saw her here, as if she'd never done anything wrong and had every right to be back in Estherville, I knew I'd made the right decision. I'd been researching private investigators, because I wanted to hire someone who knew what they were doing, when Veronica told me Richard died!" Grace flushed and her eyes narrowed. Maddie wondered if she was reliving that scene.

"What were you going to do if you found him?" Maddie asked.

"I was going to beg him to leave Veronica and come back to Estherville with me," Grace replied. "The reason I hadn't searched for him before now was I couldn't believe he'd left me for Veronica in the first place, even if my father had threatened him.

Back then I thought we could run away together after my father pointed a gun at him. Richard knew I was going to college, and we could have lived together in a small apartment off campus. He could get a job and my father was giving me a small allowance, so we would have managed just fine. And then when I graduated and got a job, I would have supported him so he could go to college. By this time I imagined we'd be married. I had it all planned in my head." She laughed bitterly.

"Why didn't that happen?" Suzanne asked curiously.

"Because—" Grace sucked in a huge breath, "—Veronica told me she stole Richard from me! She said those exact words! I was so shocked all I could stammer was, why? And she said after my father threatened Richard, she found him in a bar, dead drunk. She took him home with her but he was too drunk to have sex with her. But she didn't care. In the morning she told him they'd slept together." Tears trickled down her face.

"He must have been so ashamed of himself. He'd always told me he didn't like her, and in fact we'd been saving ourselves for each other. And then—" she sucked in another breath, "—Veronica told me she lied to him and told him he got her pregnant! That was why he ran off with her. Not because he fell in love with her but because she tricked him! No wonder I never saw him again."

"Is that when you …" Maddie trailed off.

"Yes. I couldn't take any more. That woman seemed to delight in taunting me about Richard. I can just imagine the sort of miserable life he must have led married to that – that – b-witch. She said they never did have any kids."

"Then what happened?" Suzanne asked breathlessly.

"I grabbed the lid of the trash can, ready to hit her over the head, but then I saw that pot. I was worried the metal lid wasn't heavy enough to do the job properly, so I reached into the can, picked up the pot and heaved it at her head with all my might. And it worked!" Grace sounded proud. "I stuffed her in the trash can because that's where she belonged. In the trash."

"And then you took the plant pot home with you," Maddie said.

"Yes. I thought I'd washed it thoroughly and then I put it in a corner of the garden, out of sight of most people—" she frowned at Maddie and Suzanne "—but where I could admire it – as long as I didn't think about what I used it for. I don't know how Trixie found that bit of … Veronica on it.

"And I would have gotten away with it too, if it weren't for you two girls." Grace glowered at them. "Veronica had upset plenty of people in Estherville before she left town with Richard. The sheriff's department would never be able to work out who did it."

"Why don't we call Detective Edgewater and tell him what happened?" Suzanne said hopefully. "I'm sure he would understand there were mitigating circumstances. You mightn't even go to jail."

Grace snorted. "I don't think so, dear. Killers go to prison. Even if a judge took pity on me, I'd still spend some years behind bars. And who would look after my garden while I was away?"

"We know someone who's a professional gardener," Maddie said

231

desperately, thinking of Genevieve, a woman they'd met a few months ago. "I'm sure she could take you on as a client while you're – you're … indisposed."

Hope flared in Grace's eyes for a second, then extinguished.

"It's too late. I don't think I'd survive prison. And how could I come back here afterward? Everyone would treat me like a pariah. My family was one of the founders of Estherville. I'm respected here. That's going to continue."

Grace grabbed Suzanne's arm. "Now I'll have to think about what to do with you two." She looked down at Trixie. "Three."

Maddie gasped.

"Don't worry, Maddie. I won't harm Trixie. I couldn't do that to her. I'll hand her in to the animal shelter and tell them I found her wandering around outside. *After* I dispose of your bodies."

Now it was Suzanne's turn to gasp.

Maddie looked at Trixie with widened eyes. If they were going to do something *magical*, now was the time.

Trixie read her mind.

Her familiar's white fur seemed to puff out around her, her silver spine and tail glowing for an instant.

A huge cloud of smoke filled the hall, making it hard to see.

"Run, Suzanne!" Maddie shouted as she and Trixie made for the front door.

Trixie's turquoise eyes glittered, acting like a flashlight so Maddie could find her way through the billowing smoke as they raced out of the house.

"What's happening?" Grace screamed.

"I'm right behind you," Suzanne panted, touching Maddie's shoulder.

Maddie flung open the front door, stumbling out onto the porch.

"Mrrow!" Trixie's voice was urgent.

"Once we're in the car we'll call Detective Edgewater," Maddie told her familiar. She scooped up Trixie and ran to the car, Suzanne on her heels.

Maddie dived into the driver's side, slamming the door shut. As soon as Suzanne jumped in, she hit the locks.

Maddie peeled away from the kerb like a getaway driver, only breathing a sigh of relief when they were a block away. She glanced over at Suzanne – her face was pale and she was still catching her breath.

Only then did Maddie realize Trixie sat quietly on her lap while she drove. Pulling over, Maddie stroked the Persian.

"Thank you." She buried her face in her familiar's lush white fur.

"Mrrow." It sounded like, *"You're welcome."*

"What happened back there?" Suzanne's color had returned. "Was the smoke you or Trixie? Because you can't do a smoke spell – can you?"

"It was Trixie." Maddie looked at her familiar in wonder.

"You're so clever, Trix." Suzanne gently stroked the cat. "Thank you."

"Mrrow," Trixie replied, her voice soft.

"We've got to phone Detective Edgewater." Maddie whipped out her cell. "I've got him!" she told Suzanne when her call was answered. She explained the situation quickly to the detective, who told them to go to the sheriff's station in Estherville and wait for him there.

"Let's go!" Suzanne said after Maddie filled her in.

Trixie hopped over to Suzanne as Maddie put the car into gear.

"I just hope no one saw Trixie in the front with us," Maddie said as she drove to the sheriff's station, more sedately this time.

"I'm sure they'd understand if we told them we were fleeing a killer!"

"Mrrow," Trixie agreed.

Once they arrived at the sheriff's department, they trooped inside and sat on hard plastic chairs in the waiting room.

"I can't believe Grace wanted to kill us." Suzanne couldn't keep the horror out of her voice.

"I know." Maddie closed her eyes as she relived the scene in the hall. She snapped them open and cast a glance around the beige painted room, but they were alone. "It's lucky Trixie thought of something to foil Grace. I thought of doing the Escape Your Enemy spell," she whispered, "but I didn't know if it would work for you as well. I've only done it once."

"We'd better make sure we take Trixie with us whenever we talk to a suspect," Suzanne replied. "Just in case."

"Perhaps there won't be any more murders," Maddie said hopefully.

"But maybe this is your destiny, Mads. Don't you think it's strange the first murder occurred just after your twenty-seventh birthday, when the book says that's when you come into your full powers?"

"One full moon at a time," Maddie reminded her.

"And one murder at a time." Suzanne giggled, then sobered. "I know I shouldn't laugh at a time like this." She shivered.

"I understand." Maddie touched her arm.

Once Detective Edgewater arrived with a handcuffed and sobbing Grace, he took their statements. Maddie and Suzanne had decided not to mention the cloud of smoke Trixie had created. Detective Edgewater would never believe them, and Suzanne was the only person who knew about Maddie and Trixie's magical powers.

"The suspect says she couldn't see anything in a fog of smoke, and that's how you were able to escape," Detective Edgewater said to Maddie at the end of her interview. "But we checked and there wasn't smoke anywhere in her house. You don't know anything about that, do you?"

"No," Maddie replied, hating the fact she was lying to him. "Maybe her guilt made her distraught and she was seeing things."

"Hmm." He made a note, then escorted the three of them out of the station. "She's confessed to killing Veronica," he told them. "I'm just glad she didn't have a chance to kill you, too."

"So am I," Suzanne said, her ponytail bouncing madly.

"Mrrow!" Trixie agreed.

"I'm glad you're okay, Trixie," the detective said with a smile. "But next time, try to persuade Maddie and Suzanne *not* to go after a killer."

EPILOGUE

The whole town of Estherville tsked and looked shocked when they found out that Grace had killed Veronica.

Grace's friends volunteered to help look after her garden, and there was talk of renting the house to a tenant who was an enthusiastic gardener, if Grace agreed. The rental income would help pay her legal fees, although according to the rumor mill, Grace was comfortably off.

Maddie was glad that the glorious garden wouldn't be neglected.

When their customers found out that Trixie had accompanied Maddie and Suzanne to Grace's house that fateful day, they made an even bigger fuss of her than usual.

Suzanne used the attention to their advantage – she created a new topping for their hot coffees – chocolate powder sprinkled on top of whipped cream, and called it The Trixie Special. It was even more popular than their iced coffee and mocha beverages!

"I still can't believe Grace murdered Veronica." Suzanne shuddered. It was eleven o'clock the following Tuesday, and they'd just run out of cream.

"I know." Maddie nodded.

"Mrrow." Trixie sounded a little sad.

They'd been busy all morning but for a few seconds there weren't any customers.

"I'll have to go to the grocery store and buy some more cream." Suzanne sank on a stool. "In a minute. My feet need a little rest."

"So do mine." Maddie sat down as well. Business had been great yesterday, too, although the reason why was distressing.

Attempting to lighten the mood, she teased, "You're not taking a detour to Ramon's salon, are you?"

"What gave you that idea?" Suzanne blushed.

"You were!" Maddie smiled.

"Oh, Mads, when Ramon found out what happened with Grace, he came over to check that I was okay. And he made me an espresso in my little machine while suggesting I go and sit on the sofa in the

living room to relax. And then we talked
– and talked."

"Is that all?" Maddie eyed her friend's
faraway expression.

"Yes! Although, I *was* hoping he
would kiss me again. And he did! Last
night after dinner at the little bistro."

"I'm so happy for you." Maddie
grinned.

"Mrrow!" Trixie sounded pleased.

"What about you and Luke?"

"He was glad we weren't hurt,"
Maddie replied.

"Uh-huh." Suzanne nodded. "I called
him on Saturday to tell him we'd solved
the murder." She bit her lip. "He was a
bit concerned."

"I hear you." Maddie had been
frazzled in the kitchen that night,
attempting to cook dinner, until Luke had
put his hand over hers and suggested they
get take out instead – and he was paying.

He'd also given her shoulders a
massage that evening while she told him
what had transpired that afternoon. She
guiltily left out the part about Trixie
making smoke appear in Grace's hall –
which had made her tenser for a few

minutes, until his gentle touch had soothed her.

She wanted to tell Luke the truth about her and Trixie, but was unsure what his reaction would be. Would he be cool about it, or would he freak out? Maybe she should talk it over with Trixie first, then trust in the strength of her and Luke's connection when she finally told him she was a witch.

After all, there was magic all around them – her relationship with Luke was proof of that.

THE END

A list of the previous books on the next page as well as a recipe for Iced Coffee!

Titles by Jinty James

I hope you enjoyed reading this mystery. Sign up to my newsletter at www.JintyJames.com and be among the first to discover when my next book is published!

Have you read:

Spells and Spiced Latte - A Coffee Witch Cozy Mystery - Maddie Goodwell 1

Visions and Vanilla Cappuccino - A Coffee Witch Cozy Mystery - Maddie Goodwell 2

Magic and Mocha – A Coffee Witch Cozy Mystery – Maddie Goodwell 3

Enchantments and Espresso – A Coffee Witch Cozy Mystery – Maddie Goodwell 4

Familiars and French Roast - A Coffee Witch Cozy Mystery – Maddie Goodwell 5

Please turn the page for the Iced Coffee recipe!

Iced Coffee Recipe

1 shot of espresso (or 2 if you like it extra strong. You can also use instant coffee mixed with hot water)

½ cup – 1 cup of cold milk, depending on taste

Ice cubes (optional)

Ice-cream (optional)

Whipped cream (optional)

Put the coffee in a heat safe glass. Stir in the milk. Add ice cubes and/or ice-cream if desired. You could also whiz up this concoction in a blender.

Add whipped cream on top if you want to be really indulgent!

Printed in Great Britain
by Amazon